Just the sight of her still stirred a desire in him like no woman ever had.

Her hair was still the color of sunshine, and he knew the feel of it between his fingers the same way he knew the feel of her skin beneath his lips.

"It was good to see you," he said. Good and painful.

"You, too, Jace." She studied him for a moment, her smile rueful.

As he watched her walk away, he felt all those old feelings rush at him like fighter planes.

He turned toward his rental SUV and told himself, as he had twelve years ago, that he would have hurt her worse if he'd married her and stayed in Whitehorse.

As he reached for his keys, he felt it again. That insane sensation that someone was watching him.

He thought for a moment that he'd imagined the feeling of being watched...but across the street was a silver SUV like the one he'd rented. And someone was sitting behind the wheel, watching his every move....

USA TODAY Bestselling Author

B.J. DANIELS

HIGH-CALIBER CHRISTMAS

HARLEQUIN®

TORONTO • NEW YORK • LONDON
AMSTERDAM • PARIS • SYDNEY • HAMBURG
STOCKHOLM • ATHENS • TOKYO • MILAN • MADRID
PRAGUE • WARSAW • BUDAPEST • AUCKLAND

This book is for E-dub of Laramie, Wyo. He knows why.

Recycling programs
for this product may
not exist in your area.

ISBN-13: 978-0-373-74561-6

HIGH-CALIBER CHRISTMAS

Copyright © 2010 by Barbara Heinlein

All rights reserved. Except for use in any review, the reproduction or
utilization of this work in whole or in part in any form by any electronic,
mechanical or other means, now known or hereafter invented, including
xerography, photocopying and recording, or in any information storage
or retrieval system, is forbidden without the written permission of the
publisher, Harlequin Enterprises Limited, 225 Duncan Mill Road,
Don Mills, Ontario M3B 3K9, Canada.

This is a work of fiction. Names, characters, places and incidents are
either the product of the author's imagination or are used fictitiously,
and any resemblance to actual persons, living or dead, business
establishments, events or locales is entirely coincidental.

This edition published by arrangement with Harlequin Books S.A.

For questions and comments about the quality of this book please contact
us at Customer_eCare@Harlequin.ca.

® and TM are trademarks of the publisher. Trademarks indicated with
® are registered in the United States Patent and Trademark Office, the
Canadian Trade Marks Office and in other countries.

www.eHarlequin.com

Printed in U.S.A.

ABOUT THE AUTHOR

USA TODAY bestselling author B.J. Daniels wrote her first book after a career as an award-winning newspaper journalist and author of thirty-seven published short stories. Since then she has won numerous awards, including a career achievement award for romantic suspense and many nominations and awards for best book.

Daniels lives in Montana with her husband, Parker, and two springer spaniels, Spot and Jem. When she isn't writing, she snowboards, camps, boats and plays tennis.

To contact her, write to B.J. Daniels, P.O. Box 1173, Malta, MT 59538 or email her at bjdaniels@mtintouch.net. Check out her website at www.bjdaniels.com.

Books by B.J. Daniels

HARLEQUIN INTRIGUE

 †Whitehorse, Montana
 *Whitehorse, Montana: The Corbetts
 **Whitehorse, Montana: Winchester Ranch
 ††Whitehorse, Montana: Winchester Ranch Reloaded

CAST OF CHARACTERS

Jace Dennison—The former rodeo cowboy turned government operative's life takes a turn when a mystery woman follows him home to Montana.

Kayley Mitchell—The elementary-school teacher had given up hoping that the man she loved would ever return to Whitehorse.

Ava Carris—She'd never gotten over the loss of her husband. Until she saw a man who reminded her of him.

Ty Reynolds—He'd always wanted what Jace Dennison had—especially his girlfriend.

McCall Winchester—The sheriff hated to give Jace Dennison the bad news.

Virginia Winchester—She's believed for thirty years that her baby had died.

Cade Jackson—He worries about his old friend Jace—and with good reason.

Eva Hart—She promised her twin she would always be there for her—even from the grave.

Chapter One

Jace Dennison saw the woman staring at him as he took a seat to wait for his flight to Montana. He immediately opened the book he'd picked up to avoid being forced to talk to anyone.

But as he did, the letter from his mother fell out. Jace felt a wave of guilt along with grief as he bent to pick it up. If only he had read it and been able to return to Montana before it was too late.

Unsteadily, he opened the envelope and pulled out the letter. What surprised him was that it wasn't one of her usual cheerful letters that ended with "I hope you can come home" for whatever birthday, holiday or other event.

No, this letter was different. There was an urgency in her words. She must have known she was dying. Jace read the letter again. Over the years, he had managed to make it home for his mother's birthday and a few other occasions…though not many, he thought with regret.

What bothered him about this letter was what his mother wasn't saying. Apparently, there was something she needed to tell him, something that had weighed heavily on her for years, making him even more convinced that she'd known she was dying. Why hadn't she let him know before it was too late?

He studied the letter and frowned. His mother almost made it sound as if she had a secret. Jace found that hard to believe. Marie Dennison wasn't the kind of woman who could keep a deep, dark secret, especially not from her only child. Not that cheerful, loving woman who'd raised him after his father had died. She'd already raised her younger brother, Audie.

But what had set off alarms was that his mother had insisted that she needed to tell him in person.

With growing regret, he realized he might never know what that secret was. When he'd landed in Miami, he'd been notified by his superior that there had been another tragedy at home. His uncle Audie Dennison had apparently been killed. The details were sketchy.

All Jace knew was that he was going home to bury the only family he had left—and he hadn't been there when they had needed him the most.

"Excuse me."

He looked up and was surprised to see it was the same woman who'd been staring at him earlier. She appeared to be close to his own age, early thirties, a petite, slight woman with dark hair cut in a chin-length bob. Her wide brown eyes had a haunted look to them in a face that was painfully beautiful.

"Excuse me," she repeated, her voice soft and apologetic. "I hate to bother you, but you look so much like my late husband. My husband's name was Carris. John Carris."

He smiled sympathetically. "No, I'm sorry. I'm afraid I've never heard the name before."

She nodded, looking disappointed. "I was so sure…" Her gaze moved over the contours of his face. "You look so much like him you could be brothers." She quickly took a step back. "My mistake. I'm sorry to have bothered you."

"It was no bother. I'm sorry to hear about

your husband." It was clear that her loss had been recent.

"Thank you." She turned and walked away.

He stared after her for a moment, sympathizing with her in a way she would never know. Several people sitting nearby had been watching him and the woman, he realized, but they soon went back to what they had been doing.

Jace glanced again at the letter he'd been reading before she'd approached him then carefully put it into his jacket pocket.

As his flight was called, he rose to join the line of people preparing to board—and hesitated. Ahead of him, the widow Carris showed the attendant her boarding pass, and Jace had the strangest sense of foreboding.

He'd stayed alive this long by trusting his instincts.

"Sir?" the man said behind him when he failed to move forward.

"Sorry," Jace said as he stepped aside to pretend to dig out his boarding pass, knowing he couldn't trust his emotions right now. Not having just recently lost not only his mother, but also his uncle. Not with that letter in his pocket worrying him.

He'd never been afraid of flying—not even

after his recent jungle crash, which had left him badly injured. He'd flown hundreds of times in planes that had looked as if they wouldn't get off the ground, into and out of countries where he wasn't welcome.

What was there to fear flying home to Montana in this 777 on such a beautiful day? Hell, it wasn't even snowing yet, and it was November.

As he watched Mrs. Carris disappear down the tunnel to the plane, the attendant announced final call for the flight to Billings, Montana.

Jace swore and did something he hoped he wouldn't regret. For the first time in years, he didn't listen to his instincts. The last time had been when he'd left the woman he had been about to marry to go to work as an undercover operative for the government.

Taking out his boarding pass, he tried not to limp as he headed for the plane unable to shake his bad feeling. As he caught up with Mrs. Carris, he hoped uncharitably that they wouldn't be sitting near each other.

The last thing he needed was to talk about death for the whole flight. He wondered idly why she was going to Montana.

As he limped down the aisle to his seat, his injured leg bothering him more all of a sudden, he couldn't help being relieved that Mrs. Carris was sitting a half-dozen seats behind him. She hadn't noticed him, busy fastening her seatbelt.

He quickly sat down and opened his book, fighting a sudden urge to flee. Jace knew this had to have something to do with what he would be facing when he got home. His supervisor had told him to stop by the sheriff's department when he reached Whitehorse. That alone had him worried as hell.

THE TAKEOFF WAS SMOOTH, the skies friendly and calm. When the plane landed on the rimrock in Billings, Montana, he breathed a sigh of relief, glad he hadn't listened to his instincts this time. Apparently there had been nothing to his earlier premonition of impending doom.

Still, as he headed for the rental-car line, he was so glad to be on solid ground that he didn't see the woman until she bumped into him.

"Sorry," they said in unison.

Mrs. Carris's laugh surprised him as he reached to pick up the carry-on she'd dropped when they'd collided. She grabbed his jacket sleeve to steady herself as she took her bag from him.

"You can't seem to get away from me," she said with a smile. "I was trying to catch you to thank you for being so understanding earlier at the Denver airport. Another man might have thought I was trying to pick him up." Her cheeks flushed, and he could practically see her bite her tongue.

"It's quite all right, Mrs. Carris."

She looked away, embarrassed, and fiddled with the wedding band she still wore.

"Ava, please. Mrs. Carris only reminds me…" Her eyes filled with tears.

"Ava," he said and extended his hand. "Jace. Jace Dennison."

She smiled as she took his hand. Hers was small, cool to the touch and surprisingly strong. "I need to go back that way," she said with a glance over her shoulder. "Thank you again for your understanding. Not all men are so… kind."

"Have a nice trip, Mrs. Carris."

"You, too." This time when she walked away, her step seemed a little lighter. He turned to the rental-car counter, silently wishing her well, thinking it was the last he would see of Ava Carris.

It wasn't until later, when he stopped for dinner on the three-hour drive north to Whitehorse, that he reached into his jacket pocket for his mother's letter only to find it gone.

Chapter Two

Ava Carris had planned to fly from Billings on to Seattle. At least that's what her ticket said. She'd gone with a cheaper ticket, which meant several stops in Montana before arriving late in Seattle.

It was John's fault. Even though her husband was gone, he was still with her in small ways. Thanks to his life insurance, she could afford to fly first class if she wanted.

But John had taught her to be frugal. Cheap, her sister would have said.

Ava swatted away the thought of her sister. She hadn't heard from Evie before she'd left, which was fine with her.

Now she watched the man who'd introduced himself as Jace Dennison. She couldn't help herself. It was like looking at John. She could pretend that it was her husband renting them a car which they would drive to wherever the young man was headed. She smiled at the thought, that ache for her husband a constant companion.

Ava knew it was silly, but she waited until she saw which model Jace Dennison rented, then rented a silver SUV just like it. She cringed to think what her sister would have said. Just because he looked so much like John...

Maybe I'm just curious.

Or don't have anything better to do.

She bristled at the thought, resenting it. She was now a widow. Of course she felt a little lost, she thought as she took the keys for her silver SUV and walked outside.

What does pretending for a little while hurt?

The day was bright, almost blinding, and she had to put her hand against the building for a moment to steady herself. The dizziness had been getting worse lately. That and the headaches.

She leaned there until she felt a little better. No hurry. It wasn't like she didn't know where Jace Dennison was headed.

Once inside the rental car, she took out the letter she'd seen him reading. She was sure it had something to do with why he was in Montana. As she read it for the third time, she wondered as he must have what it was his mother was so desperate to tell him.

A secret.

How she despised secrets.

Ava rubbed her temples as she studied the return address again. Whitehorse, Montana. She'd have to buy herself a map, she thought as she started the car.

You shouldn't have taken his letter. You had no right.

She smiled bitterly. A woman had every right. John hadn't fooled her. Neither would this man who looked so much like him that it had almost stopped her heart as dead as John's when she'd seen him.

Some men were just too handsome. John Carris had been one of them. Jace Dennison was another.

Men like that you needed to keep an eye on. Who knew what kind of trouble they could get into?

Ava knew, and that was why she was headed for Whitehorse.

As Jace drove into Whitehorse, he was amazed that the small Western town never seemed to change. There were the same businesses along the main drag as there had been when he was a boy.

He'd thought he would get back to see his mother and uncle more, but his work had kept him away. At least that had been his excuse. When he had come home, he'd sneaked into town, usually late at night, and stayed out at the ranch with his mother and uncle, making a point not to see anyone.

Jace didn't fool himself about why he'd done that as he pulled into a parking spot in front of the sheriff's department, turned off the key and sat for a moment. He didn't know why he'd been told to contact the sheriff, but he did know that whatever the reason, it wasn't going to be good.

Could it have something to do with the secret his mother had hinted at in her letter? It still bothered him that he'd lost it.

The trepidation he was feeling surprised him. Fear was no stranger to him. It came with his dangerous job. But the kind of fear he was feeling now was something new. He didn't want to know what his mother might have kept from him, and the last thing he wanted was to have to bury both his mother and uncle.

Bracing himself, he opened his door and got out. It was one of those clear, incredibly blue, sunny days that Montana was famous for in the fall. A blessing of a day, because it was November. Within hours it could be snowing and cold.

Jace breathed in the smell of autumn and realized he'd forgotten this scent that was as unique as this part of Montana.

At the dispatcher's office, he was told that the sheriff was in her office. He found it down the hall.

"I guess I have been gone a long time," Jace said when he saw McCall Winchester behind the desk wearing a sheriff's uniform. "A woman sheriff in Whitehorse?" Let alone a Winchester. Although he didn't voice that sentiment, McCall picked up on it.

"No one else wanted the job." She smiled as she got to her feet and held out her hand. He and McCall had gone to high school together, though she was a few years behind him.

"We've been looking for you," she said after shaking his hand and offering him a seat. "I'm sorry about your mother's passing and your uncle Audie's."

"I know mother's was cancer, but Audie?" he asked, getting right to the point.

"Quite a bit has been going on," McCall said and hesitated. "Your uncle took his own life."

Jace sat back, although this didn't come as a complete surprise. "I knew that it would be hard on him without my mother, but…"

"There was a little more to it than that." The sheriff shifted in her seat.

"Just hit me with it," he said, afraid it had something to do with his mother's letter—and her alleged secret.

"Actually, it goes back thirty years," McCall said. "Back to the night you were born. There was another baby born within minutes of you."

A chill snaked up his spine. "You aren't going to tell me that the babies somehow got switched by mistake."

"No. Not by mistake."

He laughed, shaking his head. This was not happening. He'd tried to imagine what his mother could have possibly had to tell him. Never in all his imagination could he have conjured up this.

"You're telling me Marie wasn't my mother?"

The sheriff nodded.

"Then who the hell—"

"The other woman in labor that night was Virginia Winchester."

"Bull," he said pushing to his feet.

"I know this is hard to hear."

"You have no idea."

McCall smiled at that. "Oh, I think I might be the one person in town who really does understand. I went for twenty-seven years wondering who I was."

Jace knew what she was saying was true. She'd been like the true black sheep of the family, since no one in the Winchester branch of the family tree acknowledged that she even existed.

"Virginia Winchester?" he said, trying to calm down.

"My aunt. She was pregnant with Jordan McCormick's son. Virginia's been gone the past twenty-seven years and has only recently returned to town."

So he was the child of Virginia Winchester and Jordan McCormick. "They weren't married?"

She shook her head. "Jordan's mother was

against the relationship. There has always been bad blood between the Winchesters and McCormicks. I have no idea why. But Joanna McCormick was afraid that once the baby was born, her son Jordan would marry my aunt. That is apparently why she paid a woman posing as a nurse to switch the babies."

Jace shook his head in disbelief. "What happened to my mother's… Marie's baby?"

"Marie had a difficult pregnancy, and an even more difficult labor, apparently," McCall said. "At her advanced age, she knew the risks. From what I've found out, she was lucky that the pregnancy didn't kill her. As it was, her baby died two days after it was born."

He closed his eyes, thinking of all the times his mother had told him about how badly she'd wanted a baby, how hard it had been and how lucky she was to get him. She'd known the babies had been switched. Maybe not at first, but later…

"I'm sorry, Jace, but Joanna McCormick confessed. So did your uncle."

His eyes flew open. "My *uncle?*"

"It's complicated," she said and waited for him to lower himself back into his chair. "I can only tell you what we've been able to piece together from the last people to see Audie alive. Thirty years ago, he'd been dating a woman posing as a nurse. He knew she was going to switch the babies and obviously must have known that Marie's baby wasn't doing well. We don't believe he knew that Joanna McCormick had already paid the woman to make the switch. When she changed her mind and switched the babies back, he…"

Jace felt his heart drop. "No."

"He killed her and switched the babies. I'm sure he did it because he knew it was his sister's last chance to have a baby. Unfortunately the woman's sister—"

"He killed her, as well?"

McCall nodded.

Jace was on his feet again, pacing the floor. He raked a hand through this thick, dark hair and swore.

"This isn't possible." Jace felt sick. He couldn't quit thinking about all the times his mother had told him that he'd been a blessing from God. Well, not exactly a blessing from God, as it turned out. "You have any proof of this?"

"Because it became a criminal investigation, the baby Virginia Winchester buried was exhumed. DNA tests confirmed that the child was Marie Dennison's."

Jace looked away. "Did my mother know?"

"It all came out after she died," McCall said. "I don't think she knew what her brother had done."

Or she'd known from that moment thirty years ago when a nurse had put the baby in her arms—and said nothing?

Jace hated to think how long she had known he wasn't the son she'd conceived. Long enough that she'd wanted to tell him before she died, of that he was certain.

"This is really a hell of a thing to drop on someone," he said. "What am I supposed to do with this information?"

McCall shook her head. "Virginia Winchester is your mother. What you decide to do with the information is up to you."

He rubbed a hand over his face.

"She's staying out at the ranch with my grandmother."

"Your *grandmother?*" He remembered stories about the reclusive Pepper Winchester. Since when had she acknowledged that McCall was her granddaughter?

McCall smiled. "Like I said, a lot has happened since you left town."

"Apparently."

"I'm sorry you had to come back to this along with everything else."

"Yeah, me, too."

"If there is anything I can do…"

"So, I guess you and I are…"

"Cousins," McCall said.

"You'll understand if I'm not excited about being a Winchester."

She smiled. "Call me if you need anything."

He left, stopping outside on the sidewalk to breathe. The news had him more than a little rattled. It was as if nothing in his past had been as he'd thought it. Not his mother. Not even his uncle Audie. Most especially, not himself.

Jace walked three doors down to the Range Rider Bar, shoved open the door and stepped into the dim, cool darkness. He needed a drink.

As he took a stool at the bar, the young female bartender smiled at him. "What would you like?"

"Beer. Whatever you have on tap." He'd never been a drinker. As she walked away, he realized he should have ordered something stronger. He glanced in the mirror behind the bar, taking in the three patrons on stools at the other end, glad to see that he didn't recognize anyone—nor did they seem to know him.

When the bartender brought his beer, he stared into the depths of his glass and tried to take in what McCall had told him.

Audie murdered two women and took his own life? He thought of his uncle, a prickly loner who only softened when he was around his sister Marie and Jace. But he would never have guessed the man capable of *murder*.

"Holy hell," he breathed and took a long drink of the beer.

Marie Dennison wasn't his mother. Instead Virginia Winchester was? He'd never laid eyes on the woman.

Nor did he plan to, he thought as he took another drink. He'd get the only mother he'd known and Audie buried. Then he would get the hell out of here.

He thought about his family ranch to the north of town, where he'd been raised. He'd put it up for sale. That way there would be no reason to ever come back here.

He finished his beer, feeling a little better.

First the mortuary, then a real estate office. With luck, he'd be putting all of this behind him in forty-eight hours.

Getting up, he tossed some money on the bar and headed for the door. As he stepped out onto the sidewalk, he came face-to-face with the only woman he'd ever loved—and the real reason he had sneaked in and out of town all these years.

MCCALL HATED THAT SHE'D had to give Jace Dennison the bad news. She was still a little shocked to see how much he looked like the rest of the Winchesters. Why hadn't they all seen it growing up? Maybe some people had seen it.

Or maybe it had taken him growing into a man to see the striking resemblance. He'd left Whitehorse at eighteen. Now he was a man, an incredibly handsome man with the Winchester dark eyes and hair.

What would he do now that he knew the truth? Get out of town as quickly as possible. As it was, he'd given Whitehorse a wide berth for years. After his father's death, he'd visited the ranch to see his mother and uncle but hadn't been seen around town.

Her phone rang. She picked up, not surprised to hear her grandmother's voice.

"Did I catch you at a bad time?" Pepper Winchester asked.

"I was just thinking about you," McCall said. "I might come down to the ranch this afternoon. Are you and Virginia going to be around?"

Her grandmother chuckled at that, since she hadn't left the ranch in twenty-seven years except recently, and that was only to help McCall pick out flowers for her wedding.

"I suppose Virginia will be here," Pepper said. "Is there something you need to talk to her about?"

"Yes, I'll be there in about an hour," McCall said. "Please don't have Enid cook anything." She hung up, thinking about her grandmother's irascible housekeeper. For all the years Pepper had been a recluse, closed up on the ranch, all she'd had for company was Enid Hoagland and her husband, Alfred.

With Alfred gone, now there was only Enid and McCall's aunt Virginia. Virginia was possibly even a worse companion, given her bitter relationship with her mother. McCall often wondered why she was still at the ranch.

Pepper was convinced her daughter was after the famed Winchester fortune, but McCall suspected Virginia had other reasons for wanting to be with her mother after all these years.

KAYLEY.

Jace looked into those amazing blue eyes of hers and was surprised that they were exactly as they were in his dreams. Her hair was still the color of sunshine, and he knew the feel of it between his fingers the same way he knew the feel of her skin beneath his lips.

"Kayley," Jace said on a breath. What was she doing here? Last he'd heard she was teaching school in some small town in western Montana.

"Jace," she said, her wide, full mouth quirking a little as if amused at his reaction to running into her. She would have expected him to return to Whitehorse for his mother and uncle's funerals, but he didn't have a clue she'd be in town, even though he should have. She and his mother had always been close.

His mother—he groaned inwardly at the thought of what the sheriff had told him.

"So you're just home for the funeral," he asked. Kayley had always been able to knock him off balance. He'd thought he'd outgrown her effect on him. It shocked him that she could still make him feel like a teenager.

She shook her head. "I live here now."

Damn, but she hadn't changed. If anything she was more beautiful. Her blond hair was shorter, her blue eyes still like the Montana sky, her wide, full mouth still entirely too kiss-able. She wore jeans, boots, a checked Western shirt and jean jacket…and no one wore jeans like Kayley Mitchell.

"I came back a year ago. I'm teaching kindergarten here in town." Her expression softened. "I was so sorry to hear about your mother. Marie was a very special person."

"Wasn't she, though." Marie had adored Kayley and had been devastated when he'd broken the engagement. While his mother had not mentioned Kayley for years, he'd known that Marie kept in touch with her. He'd seen a letter to Kayley at his mother's house the last time he was in town. That's how he knew she was teaching in Western Montana. It had been addressed to her at the school.

He'd wondered then if his mother had left the letter out where he could see it. The address had been Miss Kayley Mitchell. Not subtle, but effective. Kayley hadn't married. At least, she hadn't been married then.

"So, you came back to Whitehorse," he said.

"This is home," she said a little defensively. "I missed it. You're still doing whatever it was you do."

"Still," he said, also feeling defensive.

They stood like that, just looking at each other, neither of them seeming to know what to say. Jace wondered why she didn't tie into him, tell him what a jackass he'd been to break things off so close to their wedding date. He deserved her anger after what he'd done to her. He thought they'd both feel better if she just let him have it.

"How are you doing?"

He shrugged. "I'm okay."

She nodded, clearly knowing he was lying. That was the problem with a woman knowing you too well.

"It's tough, you know, with everything that came with Marie's death."

"Marie?" She raised an eyebrow. "She was still your mother no matter what."

"Yeah." And Audie was still his uncle, and

everyone in the county knew his life history even before he did.

"I know it was hard for you to come back," she said.

He almost laughed, because he was just wishing to hell he hadn't. Seeing Kayley made it all worse. If that plane crash had laid him up just a little longer in the jungle…

"If you need any help, or just someone to talk to, for old time's sake," she said, "I bought my folks' place. If you don't remember the phone number, it's in the book. They moved to Arizona, spend most of the year there and some with my sister in California, only a month here in the summer." She stopped abruptly.

He figured she knew he wasn't going to call.

"My thoughts will be with you tomorrow," she said.

"It was good to see you," he said. Good and painful. All these years, he'd tried to convince himself that he'd gotten over her. No wonder he'd gone out of his way on his other visits back home to make sure he didn't run into her.

"You, too, Jace." She studied him for a moment, her smile rueful.

As he watched her walk away, he felt all those old feelings rush at him like fighter planes. He swore under his breath, wishing she'd told him what a bastard he was instead of offering to help him through the next few days.

Just the sight of her still stirred a desire in him like no woman ever had.

As he turned toward his rental SUV, he told himself as he had twelve years ago that he would have hurt her worse if he'd married her and stayed in Whitehorse. But even as he told himself that, he couldn't get one thought out of his mind. What if he hadn't left? What if he'd stayed and married her? Hell, they could have a couple of kids by now.

That struck him like an arrow to the heart. He stopped as he reached the SUV and was reaching for his keys, when he felt it again. That insane sensation that someone was watching him.

He realized with a sobering shock that normally he was more aware of his surroundings. It was a survival skill in his business. But he'd been so shaken up over everything since getting his mother's letter and the news of her death and his uncle's that he'd gotten sloppy.

Now, though, he took in the street. On this side was a row of businesses, a half-dozen pickups parked diagonally in front of them. An elderly woman came out of the hardware store. A man went into the bank at the end of the block. A car came up the street.

He thought for a moment that he'd imagined the feeling of being watched. He'd already realized that he couldn't trust his instincts earlier with that moment of panic before he'd boarded the plane.

But his instincts told him that he wasn't so out of it that he'd imagined this.

His gaze fell on a silver SUV like the one he'd rented. It was parked across the street by the park. Someone was sitting behind the wheel, but with the sun glinting off the window...

A pickup went by, casting a long shadow over the SUV across the street. That's when he saw her. She wore large sunglasses and a hat. She quickly looked away, but he'd recognized her. As he started to cross the street, she hurriedly started the engine and took off, her face turned away. But there was no doubt.

The woman driving the SUV was the woman he'd met at the airport. Ava Carris. What was she doing in Whitehorse? Or maybe more to the point, why was she sitting on the main drag watching him?

Chapter Three

Kayley Mitchell climbed into her pickup, telling herself she was fine. But after several attempts to put her key in the ignition, she gave up and quit pretending, letting the tears come. Jace.

She'd known seeing him again would be hard. She'd thought she was ready to face him. She'd been wrong. Nothing had prepared her for this, even though she'd known he would come home for his mother's funeral—if he could.

But then Jace had been running from his feelings for years. Could she really be sure what he would do? Especially now after hearing about not only his mother's death, but also his uncle's suicide and all that that entailed.

The story was all over town. Her friend and local reporter Andi Jackson had finally done an article about the murders, the baby switch and how Jace Dennison was actually the son of Virginia Winchester. It was all anyone had been talking about for the past month.

Kayley could just imagine how hard all of this was on Jace. She knew seeing her didn't make things easier for him. Did he think she didn't know that he seldom came home even to see his mother and uncle, and, when he did, he avoided town? Avoided even the chance he might run into her if she was home visiting?

She had thought for sure that he would come home when he heard about his mother's illness. But he hadn't, so she had begun to doubt he would show up for her funeral—until she came out of the store, and there he was.

It had taken her breath away. She was still trembling inside. One look at him and she saw that he'd heard about his uncle. Her heart had gone out to him, even as badly as he'd hurt her. He'd lost his mother and uncle. As far as she knew, he had no other family.

Kayley brushed angrily at her tears. She felt just as she had in high school, her heart pounding, pulse racing, mouth dry as cotton. Hadn't she cried enough tears for Jace Dennison? He'd broken her heart and she'd never gotten over it. It had taken everything in her not to let him see the effect he had on her.

Not that she ever wanted him to know how much he'd hurt her. Twelve years had dulled the pain but done nothing to temper the desire she still felt for him. She'd moved on, and yet just seeing him had brought it all back, the memory of the two of them together.

She looked around now, afraid she'd been seen crying over him, or, worse, that Jace had witnessed it. Everyone in town would be talking about the two of them as it was. She didn't need them gossiping about her breakdown on the main drag.

But as she glanced around, she didn't see Jace. Still, she felt as if someone was watching her.

AVA HAD PANICKED WHEN she'd seen Jace coming across the street toward her car. That had her less upset than the fact that he'd somehow known she was sitting across the street watching him. He'd *sensed* her.

She'd seen the way he'd looked up, suddenly aware of her. That alone told her she'd been right to follow him to Whitehorse. She'd felt a connection the first time she'd seen him at the

Denver airport. It wasn't just that he looked so much like her deceased husband, John. Something else was going on. She could feel it.

Ava had seen him talking to that woman. That was why she'd driven around the block after her close encounter with Jace. She'd been curious about the woman, picking up something in the way they'd stood as they talked to each other. There was a history there. She could feel it.

She'd gotten around the block in time to see the woman climb into a pickup. Parking, she'd watched her, seen her start to leave, then drop her head to her steering wheel. Even from a few vehicles away, Ava could see that the woman was crying.

Just as she'd thought. There had been something between this woman and Jace.

Ava tried not to hate her. But she knew the type. Blond, blue-eyed, girl next door. A cute little cowgirl. What was the story between the two of them? she wondered as she watched her finally start her vehicle and pull out.

Ava pulled out behind her, following her through town, then north into the country. It was one of those beautiful blue-skied days, the sun coming warm through her windows.

She knew she shouldn't even be in Whitehorse, let alone following this woman, and yet it felt right.

Something had brought her here, something more than Jace Dennison.

Ahead, the cowgirl slowed, then turned down a narrow road. Ava could see a farmhouse set back against a hillside. Several large old cottonwoods framed the picturesque place.

How handy, Ava thought as she realized that this woman lived just down the road from Jace Dennison—according to the address on the letter from his mother.

Ava drove on past, turned around up the road and headed back to town. She slowed just enough at the mailbox on the highway in front of the cowgirl's house to read the name. K. Mitchell.

She chose a motel on the far edge of town. In the room, she pulled out a phone book. There was only one Mitchell listed. Kayley Mitchell.

Ava was more convinced that the woman wasn't married. Didn't the woman know that most women living alone didn't put their full names in the phone book?

Apparently Kayley thought she was safe living out there all by herself.

While she had the phone book open, she looked up Dennison. She found two numbers, one for an Audie Dennison and another for Marie, the same name as the one on Jace's letter from his mother. She memorized the phone number for his mother before closing the book.

JACE WAS MORE DETERMINED than ever to get out of town as quickly as possible. After he'd watched Ava Carris drive away, he'd turned back and saw the *Milk River Examiner* office.

He'd heard that the editor-owner of the paper had written an obit for both Marie and Audie. He was just waiting for Jace's approval before running it. Marie had gone to school with the man, and Jace knew he was just trying to make things easier for him.

As he stepped inside, Jace spotted a young woman on the phone. She had a Southern accent, and when she turned toward the door, she seemed surprised and a little wary.

"Is Mark Sanders around?" Jace asked as the woman hung up.

"He's out on calls," she said, definitely looking nervous. "I'm the reporter, Andi Jackson. The newspaper's only reporter."

Jace blinked. "Jackson. Are you…"

"Cade's wife."

Cade Jackson, his one-time best friend. "It's nice to meet you, I think. I'm—"

"Jace Dennison." She swallowed. "I was the one who wrote the stories about you."

He'd figured Mark would have tried to keep it out of the newspaper. But apparently Cade's wife had written about it anyway.

"Everyone in town was talking about it," she said. "The rumors were worse than the truth." She'd been staring at him and now shook her head. "How could anyone not have known you were a Winchester?"

Apparently quite a few people knew. "I'd like to see the papers."

She nodded and went into the back, returning after only a few minutes. "I heard you were back. I have them ready for you. Also, there are the obits Mark wrote."

Jace reached for his wallet.

"They're on me," she said.

He thought she might apologize for putting his life on the front page of his hometown newspaper. When she didn't, he said, "You were just doing your job, right?"

"Yes," she said raising her chin. "And I'm damned good at it."

Jace had to smile. He liked her, which surprised the hell out of him. Cade had done all right. "I like a woman who stands up for what she believes in," he said and gave her his cell phone number. "Tell your husband hello for me."

As Jace left, he glanced across the street, half expecting to see Ava Carris parked on the other side again. But there was no sign of her. He felt an uneasiness as he climbed into the SUV and headed out of town. Maybe there was a reasonable explanation for what she was doing in town and why she was driving a vehicle apparently identical to the one he'd rented.

He glanced over at the newspapers on the seat next to him. One of the headlines caught his eye, and he quickly looked away. Was he really up to reading them?

It dawned on him that Ava Carris could be a reporter who hoped to mine his story further. She could have made up that story about him looking like her husband.

Or she could be a private detective working for the Winchesters.

Neither seemed likely when he thought about the petite, slight woman. But he planned to make a point of asking her the next time he saw her. And he feared there was a damned good chance he'd be seeing her again.

McCall drove out to the Winchester ranch, needing to bring the news in person. She hadn't seen her grandmother since Pepper had come into town to help her pick out flowers for the wedding.

The wedding was now just weeks away. McCall couldn't believe how quickly the time had gone. A Christmas wedding for her and Luke at Winchester ranch. Sometimes she had to pinch herself. It hadn't been that long ago that she'd never set foot on the ranch, never seen her grandmother, never been accepted as a Winchester.

Nor had it been that long ago that Luke wasn't in her life. But he'd come back to town, taken the game-warden job and started building a house south of town with apparently only one goal in mind—getting her back.

McCall smiled, glad the man was persistent.

She couldn't wait to marry him. Her only hesitation was that her grandmother might have an ulterior motive in wanting her to get married at the ranch. That and just the thought of her grandmother and mother in the same room.

She pushed those thoughts aside now as she drove under the wooden arch that read Winchester Ranch. Just over the hill she slowed, never tiring of seeing the massive ranch lodge. It was built much in the same fashion as the Old Faithful Lodge in Yellowstone Park and looked of that era.

As she parked and got out, she noticed that her grandmother's old Blue Heeler didn't get up, didn't even growl, as she walked to the door. The dog just watched her as if uninterested.

Before she could knock, Enid opened the door. Her sour look was more accusing than usual.

"It's been hell here," the old housekeeper snapped. Enid was one of those broomstick–thin, brittle old women with a nasty disposition.

Everyone in the family wondered why Pepper Winchester kept her on. Most figured Enid had something she held over the matriarch's head—and they didn't want to know what it was.

"Pepper and Virginia have been at each other's throats," Enid said as she led the way inside.

Nothing new there, McCall thought. From down a long hallway, she heard the sound of her grandmother's cane tapping on the old hardwood flooring.

Pepper Winchester was a tall, regal-looking woman. What had struck McCall the first time she'd seen her was how much she resembled her grandmother. Since then she'd seen photographs of Pepper at her age. There had been little doubt that McCall was a Winchester.

As usual, her grandmother had her salt-and-peppered dark hair pulled back in a braid that snaked over one shoulder. What was unusual was that her grandmother wasn't wearing black.

For the past twenty-seven years, Pepper had been a recluse, locked away in this big place with just Enid and Enid's husband, Alfred. Her grandmother had worn black the entire time.

Today, though, she wore jeans, a Western shirt and moccasins. She looked younger than her seventy-two years and actually smiled as she approached.

"I'm sure Enid complained to you," she said as she motioned toward the lodge parlor.

A small fire burned there, taking the chill off the November day. McCall took one of the leather chairs and watched her grandmother lower herself into the other one in front of the fire.

"How is Aunt Virginia?" McCall asked.

Pepper made a face. "Angry, sad, bitter. Pretty much what you would expect."

McCall thought of Jace's reaction to the news. "Jace Dennison is back in town for his mother's and uncle's funerals."

"You told him?"

McCall nodded. "He didn't take it well."

Pepper chuckled. "He wasn't glad to be a Winchester?" she asked with a wry smile. "Imagine that."

"I doubt he'll be in town long. Just long enough to get his business done, and then he'll be gone, probably for good."

Pepper nodded. "I have no idea what Virginia is thinking. She's still angry at me. All these years she suspected I had something to do with her baby dying."

"I'm sorry."

"You suspected that I had something to do with the babies being switched."

McCall didn't deny it. "I can't imagine what I would be feeling if I found out that the child I gave birth to didn't die but is alive—and thirty years old."

"Marie will always be Jace's mother," Pepper said.

"Don't you think Virginia wants to see him? I could talk to her."

"Talk to me about what?" Virginia said from the doorway. She was tall like her mother, with the Winchester dark coloring, but lacked Pepper's beauty at her age.

"Jace Dennison is in town for the funerals," Pepper said to her daughter.

Virginia's gaze settled on McCall. "You've seen him?"

"He's definitely a Winchester."

"Handsome?" she asked almost hopefully.

"Very. Stubborn. Independent. And probably impatient just like all the Winchesters," McCall said.

Virginia smiled ruefully. "You're trying to tell me that he isn't going to want to see me."

"It isn't up to him," Pepper snapped. "Do what you want. Just don't expect miracles."

"Thank you, Mother," she said sarcastically.

When McCall looked up, Virginia was gone. She got to her feet. "I should get back to town."

"I'm glad you took my advice and ran for sheriff."

McCall laughed. "No one else wanted the job." She studied her grandmother. "Why does it matter so much to you?"

"I told you. You're good at what you do. The county needs someone like you."

McCall wasn't so sure about that. "Does this desire you have for me to be sheriff have anything to do with my father's death?"

"We would have never known he was murdered if it wasn't for you," her grandmother said. "One of his killers is dead because of you."

McCall caught the "one of his killers." "We don't know that his killer didn't act alone."

Her grandmother gave her an impatient look. "Don't we?"

McCall sighed. "What are you planning to do?"

"Nothing. I know you will find out the truth. That's why you make such a good sheriff."

McCall looked at her grandmother and saw there was no reason to waste her breath arguing with her. So she just picked up her hat, kissed her grandmother on her cheek and left.

But as she drove away, she couldn't help but glance back in her side mirror. Her grandmother stood at the door, watching her leave, an expression of determination etched into the woman's weathered face.

Pepper Winchester was a force to be reckoned with, and she was convinced that someone in her family had betrayed her—and was a coconspirator in her youngest son's murder. Clearly, she wouldn't rest until she found out the truth.

McCall feared what that truth would do to her grandmother.

JACE QUICKLY FORGOT about Ava Carris. Running into Kayley after all these years had him reeling. She'd been the love of his life.

Back in high school he'd thought she always would be. All he'd wanted was to marry her. They'd already started their family—Kayley had been a couple of months pregnant.

He had been so excited about being a father.

Then tragedy had struck. His father died. Two weeks later, Kayley lost the baby. It shattered his picture of the future. Suddenly all that loss had changed everything. Jace knew he had been running from all that pain when he'd left Kayley, left Whitehorse.

He'd hated himself for running out on her, knowing she was in as much pain as he was. But he'd desperately needed space and time. He'd joined the Marines and later left to join an undercover special-ops government program.

He hadn't looked back. He couldn't let himself.

The familiar drive north along the Milk River through a landscape devoid of all color seemed surreal. Winter up here meant a monochromatic palette, everything dulled somewhere between white and brown. The drab landscape mirrored his feelings. He would get his mother and uncle buried; then he would put all of this behind him.

He hadn't gone far when he spotted the mailbox with Dennison on it and slowed to turn down the tree-lined narrow dirt road. The house was an old two-story farmhouse, white with blue shutters.

His treehouse was still in one of the largest old cottonwoods down by the creek. A tire swing hung from one of the larger branches. It moved restlessly in the breeze, reminding him of summer days spent daydreaming in it.

As he pulled in, nothing moved. He half expected his mother to appear in the front doorway. Marie, he thought with no small amount of resentment. She wasn't the only thing missing. No dog. Jace figured a neighbor must have taken his uncle Audie's collie. No Audie, either.

He sat for a moment, swamped with memories of a childhood free to wander in the fields and river bottom that ran for miles behind it. A childhood with the little girl who lived down the road.

"It hasn't all been bad, has it?" Kayley had asked him that last day before he left twelve years ago.

"No," he'd said. It hadn't been bad at all. Just the ending.

Getting out, he grabbed the overnight bag he'd brought and walked toward the house where he'd grown up. He wasn't surprised that the front door wasn't locked or that the house was spotless. His mother had always kept it that way. He took his bag up to his room.

His mother had left it just as it had been. He stood for a moment in the doorway, before moving down the hall to the guest room.

As he dropped his bag on the double bed, he stepped to the window to look out. He could see his uncle's house down the road. He would have to sell it, as well.

Back downstairs, he checked the fridge. One of the neighbors must have cleaned it out, just as they had probably been keeping the house up.

He stood for a moment in the empty house and listened, hearing nothing but his own breathing until he couldn't take it anymore and headed for town. He'd go to the grocery store to stock up on just enough food to last him until he could get the hell out of here.

AVA HAD SPOTTED THE STACK of local newspapers in the office when she'd checked into the motel on the edge of town. They had been piled next to a fireplace, no doubt to be burned.

She'd gone back after she'd settled into the room and asked the girl at the motel desk if she could look at them. Methodically, Ava had gone through them, reading the articles. She was interested in Whitehorse, this town where Jace Dennison was from.

But she was also interested in anything about Kayley Mitchell.

The newspapers went back a good couple of months. Fortunately, they were only a few pages, so it didn't take long to work her way through them.

She hadn't gone far when she found a photograph of Miss Kayley Mitchell and her kindergarten class. The cowgirl was an elementary-school teacher? Could she look any sweeter standing there with an arm around two little girls in her class?

Ava wadded up the paper and sailed it across the room before continuing her search. She was shocked when she found the front-page story about two babies being switched at the hospital thirty years before—and how a recent murder tied in. Jace Dennison had been one of the switched babies!

The thought gave her chills. She kept reading, completely engrossed and even more convinced coming here had been destined. Jace needed her.

When she found the funeral notice for Marie and Audie Dennison in the most recent newspaper, she saw that the funeral was tomorrow. She was so glad she hadn't missed it. She glanced toward her clothes hanging in the closet and smiled. How providential that she still had the black dress she'd worn to her husband's funeral.

JACE WAS STANDING IN the grocery store checkout aisle when he saw her. "Ava?"

She jumped at the sound of her name, and he thought for a moment she might run out of the store.

He stepped out of line to block her exit just in case she thought about taking off again.

"Jace? Jace Dennison, right?" she said quickly, getting her composure back.

"I thought that was you," he said, not buying for a moment that she didn't quite remember his name.

She'd been looking down another aisle when he'd spotted her, as if searching for something. Or someone.

"I hadn't realized we were headed for the same town in Montana," he said.

"Small world, isn't it."

Not that small. "Are you here alone?" he asked, glancing down the same aisle she had been looking down even though he suspected he was the person she'd been looking for.

"Yes. That is, I'm in town visiting some friends." She seemed flustered.

"Oh, who are you visiting? I know most everyone around here," he said. It wasn't quite true. He'd been gone so long that he hadn't recognized anyone since he'd been in town. Except for Kayley. And McCall.

"My friends aren't from Whitehorse," she said. "They're just passing through, so I decided to meet them up here. They love dinosaurs, and with the Leonardo museum nearby... We're all staying at the same motel. I was just getting a few snacks for later."

He saw that she had a small basket. In it were crackers and a wedge of cheese. He realized that there might be some truth to her story. It made more sense than what he'd been thinking, that was for sure.

"I personally am not that interested in fossils," she said, smiling. "I'm sure you've been to the museum."

"Yes." He'd forgotten how small and delicate she was. A wisp of a woman. Certainly no threat. And certainly no reporter or private investigator. Just a lonely widow with a lot of time on her hands.

"I think you'll enjoy it," he said, realizing just how unreliable his instincts were since hearing of his mother's death—and all the news that followed. "The other museum is just across the parking lot. It has a lot of Montana history. That might be more to your liking."

"Thank you. I'll make sure I see it."

"Well, enjoy your visit," he said and got back in line. Ava disappeared down the aisle. Once outside, he climbed behind the wheel of the SUV, started the engine and glanced back.

Had he expected to see Ava Carris watching him from inside the store?

She was nowhere in sight.

Shaking off his earlier crazy thoughts about her stalking him, he drove away.

Chapter Four

Ava knew it was just a matter of time before her sister found out she hadn't flown to Seattle as she'd planned. She'd seen the message this morning when she'd checked her cell phone, but she'd been avoiding calling her sister back.

A mistake. It would only make Evie more determined to know what was going on. The last thing she needed was her sister butting into things. Now, still shaken after running into Jace Dennison, Ava moved to the back of the store and dug out her cell phone, deciding the best way to head off trouble was to call Evie back.

She and Evie were so close they could finish each others' sentences. She'd always feared that Evie could read her thoughts. That fear was realized when Evie answered on the first ring and demanded, "Who is he?"

"It isn't always about a man," she said defensively.

"With you it is. You're going to make a fool of yourself."

"No. It isn't like that."

"So, what is it like?" her sister asked snidely.

Ava wasn't sure.

Evie heard her hesitate. "Where are you? I'm coming there."

"No. I need to be on my own for a while."

"John wouldn't want you to be alone."

She hated it when Evie brought up John. She missed him so much. "I'm not alone. I have to go. Please, just stay away."

John hadn't liked it when Evie had shown up shortly after they'd gotten married. She was always there, butting in, causing trouble.

"She's my *sister.* What do you want me to do?" Ava used to plead with him.

"I can't deal with you *and* your sister." He would storm off, and she would plead with Evie to give her some space.

But would Evie listen?

"Ava?" Evie had that patient tone that meant

she wasn't going to give up. "Tell me where you are. You know I'll find you. Why make it more difficult for me and put me in a foul mood when I see you?"

She sighed, knowing it was true. She could never get away from Evie. It had always been that way.

"I'm in Whitehorse, Montana, but I don't want you to come here." Evie wouldn't like what she was doing. "Please, Evie."

She hung up and remembered the quart of orange juice she'd seen Jace Dennison had in his grocery basket. She could almost taste it as she found the refrigerated aisle and bought herself a quart of juice just like his.

VIRGINIA WINCHESTER HAD always thought that her life would have been so different if her baby had lived.

But in reality she wasn't all that convinced things would have turned out for the better.

The father of her baby hadn't jumped at marrying her when she'd told him she was pregnant. She'd been convinced he would, though, once the baby was born and he saw his precious son.

Jordan McCormick never even saw the baby

before the son they'd conceived had died. Nor had he attended the funeral.

At the time, Virginia had blamed his mother for keeping him away. Now she wondered if he'd known what his mother had done and that the baby Virginia had buried wasn't his. Wasn't it possible he'd known all along that Marie Dennison was raising his child?

That would mean that Joanna McCormick had told her son that she'd paid someone to switch the babies.

Virginia felt a surge of anger and frustration at the thought. Maybe everyone had known but her. Now there was no way of knowing. Jordon had died in a ranching accident not long after that, and his mother was in prison, not talking after a plea bargain that got her life instead of the death sentence.

Jordan, Virginia now realized, would have never married her. His mother wouldn't have allowed it—just as her own mother had told her.

And even if he'd gotten up the gumption to stand up to his mother and do right by Virginia, she knew Joanna would never have allowed her son to stay on the ranch, let alone live there with Virginia and the baby.

Just as Virginia's own mother would never have allowed her and Jordan on the Winchester ranch. Joanna McCormick and Pepper Winchester hated each other. Virginia knew only what she'd heard through the county grapevine, but apparently her mother had been in love with Joanna's husband, Hunt McCormick.

Nothing had come of it, but still all that bad blood had spilled over onto their children.

Jordan had never been strong enough to stand up to his mother. Virginia wasn't any better with her own mother. So what would have happened to her and her son?

Any way she looked at it, Virginia knew she would have ended up raising their son alone. She had barely been able to take care of herself when her mother had thrown all of them off the ranch three years later.

She had seen how her brothers had struggled without money or a place to live after growing up being taken care of on the Winchester ranch. They'd been forced to get jobs just as Virginia had. At least she hadn't had a baby to support and care for, as well.

Her mother had asked her why she'd come back here. It wasn't out of love for her mother. She hadn't known why she'd come back.

Pepper was convinced it was for the Winchester money, but then her mother always thought the worst of her children. Except for her youngest son, Trace.

Virginia had never known what it was like to love a child so much that you could turn your back on everything and everyone else, including your other children.

Or love a child so much that when you lost him you would lock yourself away for twenty-seven years as her mother had done.

Virginia had never known that kind of love. Not for the child she thought she'd lost or for the man she'd thought she loved enough to have a child with him.

But like her mother, she'd let the past keep her isolated in other ways from the world.

And now to find out that her child hadn't died. That her son was alive and well and in town….

She had to see him, she thought as she dressed for the funerals of Marie and Audie Dennison. She knew no one in town would expect her to attend. She didn't know Marie or her brother.

But she wanted to see her son.

THE WEATHER CHANGED THE night before the funeral. Jace woke to dull skies and a wind that whipped the bare branches on the cottonwoods outside the guest bedroom.

He'd grown up in this house, knew every creak and groan, but now it felt too quiet. Not that he believed in ghosts, but he now had the strange feeling that he wasn't alone here.

That kind of thinking made him all too aware that he wasn't himself. He'd actually thought Ava Carris had followed him to Whitehorse.

He showered and went downstairs to put on the coffee. From the refrigerator he took out the quart of orange juice he'd bought at the store, unscrewed the cap and took a long drink. As he put it back in the fridge, he saw a pickup coming up the road.

He didn't recognize it, but then why should he? He'd been gone so long no one drove the same rigs they had. To his surprise, Kayley Mitchell climbed out and walked toward the house.

Glancing down, he realized that he was wearing only jeans, his chest and feet bare. He thought about making a run upstairs to get a shirt, but she was already at the door.

What did she want? He swore. He was about to find out.

Moving toward the door in anticipation of her knock, he heard her put something down, then turn and go back down the steps. He started to open the door, but she was already sliding behind the wheel of her truck.

He stared after her as she drove off, wondering why she hadn't bothered to knock. Maybe she hadn't wanted to see him. Jace was thankful for that. It would have been awkward, to say the least.

Still, it seemed odd, and he waited until her pickup turned onto the highway at the end of the drive and disappeared before he opened the door to see what she'd left.

A note was taped to the foil covering the casserole dish lying just outside the door.

This used to be your favorite. I hope it still is.
Kayley

One whiff of the casserole brought with it a wave of memories that threatened to drown him. Kayley used to make this all the time for him back when they were engaged. She'd gotten the recipe from his mother. Marie, he corrected with a scowl as he brought the dish inside and closed the front door.

It wasn't long before more people began to arrive with food. Fortunately, he'd gotten dressed after Kayley left. He'd forgotten how the community came together when there was a death.

"A lot of people loved your mother," a neighbor told him when she dropped off chicken and dumpings and a pan of brownies.

"Marie will be missed," the woman said, her voice breaking.

Jace couldn't help feeling touched by their love and generosity. But what was he supposed to do with all this food? They must think he was staying around for a while. The thought made him reach for the phone book.

He dialed a local Realtor, a girl named Clare whom he'd gone to school with, and had her list the two houses and the land. "I'll also need to sell off the livestock, so maybe you know someone I could talk to about that?"

She did. But she wasn't encouraging about selling the place quickly. "I'm afraid not much is selling right now," Clare told him.

"Just get me what you can," he said and hung

up as another neighbor drove up. He went out to help her carry in fried chicken and potato salad.

At least he wouldn't go hungry.

AT THE CEMETERY, WIND whipped what leaves hadn't already blown away. They scattered across the neatly mowed yellowed grass, making a rustling sound as the bare cottonwood limbs groaned overhead.

The air smelled of fall as Jace climbed out of his pickup. It was a scent like no other he'd experienced since he'd left here and added to the nostalgic melancholy he'd been feeling since his return.

A crowd had already gathered around the grave sites. He was thankful that he'd opted for a graveside ceremony only. He knew he couldn't have taken being closed in by all the people crammed in the mortuary building.

He couldn't believe he was burying his mother and uncle. He didn't give a damn what anyone said, but he would always think of Marie as his mother. He didn't care if the sheriff had DNA proof. He sure as hell wasn't a Winchester, nor would he ever be one.

As he started toward the two covered holes

that had been dug in the ground after the earth had been heated enough to dig, Jace tried not to think about any of it. All he had to do was get through this day.

He thought of his mother. She'd finally gotten him home. He felt his eyes burn, his heart aching. If only he could have gotten home in time to see her just once more before she died.

He had no doubt what she would have wanted to tell him. The thought broke his heart. He knew he wouldn't have handled her deathbed confession well and was thankful it hadn't happened.

It had been enough of a shock to hear it from the sheriff. This way, he would never know just how much Marie had known about the baby switch or if she'd had a part in it. And she would never know how angry he was with her and his uncle for keeping this secret from him all these years.

As the caskets were removed from the hearses, he watched his uncle's being lifted and thought of Audie. Everyone always said he would have done anything for his older sister. Well, he'd proved that, Jace thought.

The attendants were removing his mother's

casket when he felt himself stop walking before reaching the crowd.

He couldn't do this. A man who could face a band of drug runners single-handedly or drop from a plane into a jungle full of wild animals and terrorists, and here he was afraid of facing his own mother's funeral. Or at least the woman he'd thought was his mother.

Out of nowhere, Kayley appeared at his side.

"It's going to be all right," she said quietly, as if sensing his urge to run like hell.

Not sensing, he thought. This woman, like no other, *knew* him.

He looked over at her, surprised she could show him any kindness at all. Didn't she realize that by being here with him, she'd get every tongue in town wagging about what a fool she was to forgive a bastard like him?

"I don't have to go with you if you'd rather—"

"Please." It was all he could say. All he had to say.

She took his arm.

His reaction to her touch surprised him. It was light, and yet he felt it through his Western-cut suit jacket, felt it clear to his heart.

She glanced at his boots, and he saw her try to hide a smile. He'd dug out his Western boots and suit to wear today. It had felt right. Maybe at heart he was still the cowboy who'd grown up in Montana rodeoing, riding fences and raising cattle.

Jace felt the sea of faces as he moved toward the open graves, Kayley at his side. She started to leave him when they reached his spot near the preacher, but he took her hand, and she stayed.

His mother's pastor gave the sermon, talking about Marie and what a wonderful, giving woman she'd been. Jace felt a deep sense of pride, thankful for this woman who'd raised him even if she hadn't been his birth mother.

The pastor said a few words about Audie and the love he had for his sister and how God would forgive him. He wondered if the woman whose mother and aunt Audie had murdered would forgive his uncle.

When it was over, a stream of people came up to tell him how sorry they were. Many of the women were crying and told him how Marie had touched their lives. At some point, the crowd finally began to disperse.

"I'll let you be alone with her," Kayley said and was gone.

He stood looking up at the branches whipping in the wind overhead for a long while before he glanced down at the graves. "Whatever you did," he whispered, "I forgive you."

When he looked up, he saw her.

Wearing a black dress, Ava Carris stood beside a large old cottonwood at the back at the edge of the cemetery. Their eyes met across the rows of gravestones. She instantly turned to leave.

Before Jace could react, a woman stepped in front of him, blocking his path.

"I'm sorry. I…I just wanted to pay my respects," she said.

"Thank you," he said distractedly as he watched Ava Carris get into her silver SUV and drive away. So she came to the funeral. There was no law against that. She was just paying her respects. So why did seeing her send a shaft of ice up his spine?

He turned back to the woman before him, finally focusing on her. She was in her early fifties, tall with dark hair, eyes as black as his own and striking features that kept her from being what was considered pretty.

Jace felt a small tremor course through him. "I just wanted…" Her voice trailed off.

He felt a lump form in his throat.

"I'm sorry," she repeated and quickly turned away.

He stared after her, knowing he'd just come face to face with Virginia Winchester. His birth mother.

ON THE WAY BACK TO THE house, Jace swung by the liquor store and bought himself a bottle of whiskey. His plan was to get stinking drunk, something he never did, but the occasion seemed to call for it.

He poured himself a drink in one of his mom's jelly glasses in the kitchen and wandered through the deathly quiet house. He tried turning on the television but quickly turned it off. He'd gone months without seeing a television and realized he could probably go a lot longer.

As he took a drink of the whiskey, he shuddered involuntarily. Memories came at him like poison darts.

Kayley. She'd saved his bacon today at the funeral. She'd known how much he needed her, and she'd stood by his side even when he hadn't stood by her when she'd needed him the most. She'd been there with the whole town knowing what he'd done to her.

The woman had more courage than he did.

Damn. He had never deserved her. Why did she have to be so nice to him? It only made him feel worse. Or maybe that was her plan. As if Kayley could ever be vindictive.

He finished his drink, unable to sit still, and realized he couldn't stay in this house any longer. Putting down his glass, he rushed upstairs to the guest room to pack. The funeral was over. He'd tell his Realtor to call him when the property sold. Maybe he wouldn't even have to come back to sign the papers. She could just fax everything to wherever he was.

The guest bedroom door was ajar, and for a moment he couldn't remember leaving it that way. But he didn't think too much about it as he pushed open the door. He couldn't be sure of anything.

His suitcase wasn't where he'd left it.

It took him a moment, though. Had he moved it without thinking? No.

He realized that anyone could have walked

right in. No one in Whitehorse locked their doors. Hell, he wouldn't even know where his mother kept the keys.

When he'd come into the house, he hadn't paid any attention, but now he ran back downstairs. He immediately noticed something he hadn't seen when he'd come in.

Someone had left one of those small fake Christmas trees in a corner of the living room. Under it was a wrapped present.

What the hell? He was sure it hadn't been there before. Or had it?

He picked up the present and shook it suspiciously. It wasn't ticking. He tore off the paper and opened the box. A shirt.

He stared it at. Definitely not his style. But it was his size.

Putting it back under the tree, he searched the rest of the house to see if anything else was missing—or added—since he'd been there.

He found his suitcase in his old bedroom. It was empty. Opening the closet, he found his clothes hanging in the closet along with some of his old Western shirts. His underwear was neatly folded in his chest of drawers.

Who? Kayley. He swore. Who else? She

hadn't just propped him up at the funeral, she'd decided to settle him in Whitehorse?

Like hell.

He stormed out of the bedroom and headed for his rented SUV.

Kayley had said she was living just down the road in her folks' old place. He saw her pickup parked out front as he turned down her road. He refused to think about all the other times he'd driven down this road, parked in front of the house and been like a member of her family.

He climbed out, stormed past her truck and pounded on the front door. Moments later the door swung open and she stood there looking surprised to see him. She'd changed from the dress she'd been wearing earlier and now wore faded jeans, a T-shirt with an old worn flannel shirt over it that could have once been his. Her feet were bare.

She frowned. "Jace?"

"What the hell do you think you're doing?"

She blinked before narrowing her gaze at him. "I beg your pardon?"

"I'm not staying in Whitehorse, and trying to move me back in here isn't going to change anything."

"Are you talking about me showing up at the funeral? I thought—"

"You know damned well that's not what I'm talking about. Stay out of my house. Stay out of my life."

He turned and stalked back to his SUV. She was still standing in the doorway, staring after him as if he was crazy.

Maybe he was. He sure felt on the edge. As he reached the highway, he knew he couldn't go back to that house. He sat at the crossroads, not knowing which way to turn, telling himself he had to get out of this town, out of this state. This trip down memory lane was killing him.

His cell phone rang. He checked the number, half expecting it to be Kayley. It was Cade Jackson, his one-time best friend and the husband of the reporter he'd met at the *Milk River Examiner* and had given his number.

"I saw you at the funeral but didn't get a chance to talk to you," Cade said. "Want to get together for a drink?"

Jace chuckled. "Boy howdy."

He heard the smile in his friend's voice as he asked, "Remember Sleeping Buffalo? I thought you might want to get out of town."

"You are right about that."

"See you there in fifteen?"

"Cade? Thanks."

SEEING HER SON HAD SHAKEN Virginia Winchester more than she wanted to admit. She'd seen the recognition in his gaze. He'd looked panicked.

"You went to the funeral?"

She turned to see her mother standing in the doorway, leaning on her cane.

"I wanted to see him," she said as she tossed her coat down on the bed.

"Well?"

"He's my son." Her voice broke. "I would think you would understand."

"He's a grown man."

She turned to look at Pepper. "How could anyone not have known? He looks like the rest of our family." She smiled. "He is so handsome and yet so…" She shook her head.

"He's home to bury his mother and uncle. Of course he looks sad."

"Not just sad. He looks as if his feet have been kicked out from under him. I felt so sorry for him."

"There is nothing you can do for him."

"I know." She sat down on the side of her bed. Her mother leaned into the doorframe. Virginia was surprised to see compassion on her mother's face.

"I missed his whole life." Her eyes burned with tears. She'd been so angry and bitter since learning the truth, but right now all she felt was heartbroken that she hadn't known her son.

"Marie did a good job of raising him. Everyone says he's a fine young man," her mother said.

"Is that supposed to make me feel better? We both know you don't think I could have done as good a job raising him."

"Marie was married and settled. But then so was I, and look how that turned out."

Virginia glanced over at her mother and saw the pain in Pepper's expression. "You don't believe Jordan would have married me, do you?"

"His mother would never have allowed it." Pepper let out a rueful chuckle. "I should know. I destroyed my own children's relationships."

"You sound almost sorry about that."

Pepper smiled. "Almost. My sons had terrible taste when it came to women."

"You *like* McCall."

"Yes. She turned out all right in spite of her genes."

Virginia laughed. "You haven't changed at all."

"Few of us do," her mother agreed.

When Virginia looked up again, the doorway was empty. Yet she felt as if that had been the first time she and her mother had ever had a civil conversation. Almost like what she considered normal mothers and daughters.

CADE WAS SITTING AT the end of the bar when Jace walked in. His friend grabbed his beer and motioned to a booth at the back.

They shook hands, and Jace felt as if it hadn't been years since they'd last seen each other as Cade ordered them a round and they sat down.

"So, what's new?" Jace asked him.

Cade grinned. "Still raising horses and running the bait shop. Got married. She said you met her. She keeps me on my toes."

Jace could see how happy he was. He remembered his mother telling him that Cade had married right out of high school but his wife had been killed in a car accident. She'd been pregnant, and it had taken years before he'd fallen in love again.

Jace had known that kind of pain. Only the woman he'd loved hadn't died. He'd deserted her.

"I was really sorry to hear about your mom and uncle," Cade said.

"Thanks."

They talked about people they'd known. Jace noticed the way Cade didn't mention Kayley.

"I saw you limping at the funeral," Cade said.

Jace thought he'd hidden it well. Obviously not. Kayley, he knew, had noticed it as well, but she hadn't said anything.

"I would have been home sooner, but I ran into a little trouble."

Cade smiled. "I know if you told me, you'd have to kill me."

"Something like that."

"You happy?" Cade asked.

Jace shrugged. He didn't think of life in terms of happy or sad, good or bad. It just was. "I'm okay."

Cade nodded.

"Has everyone always known about me?" Jace had to ask.

"Hell, Jace, you look just like the Winchesters. I'm surprised someone didn't put it together years ago. Maybe they did and just kept quiet about it. Everyone loved Marie and was so happy for her that she had you."

"I saw my birth mother earlier at the funeral. Virginia Winchester." Jace swore and finished his beer.

"I heard she was back in town. It doesn't have to change anything."

He laughed. "Right. If you find out tomorrow that you're not a Jackson, that won't change anything."

"It would just mean I could stop trying to live up to my brother Carter," Cade joked.

"It was just a lot to be hit with. Audie…"

"That did come as a shock. I'm sure he felt he was protecting his sister."

Jace shook his head. "It's as if everything I believed was a lie."

"You know my old man married Lila Bailey, Chester's ex-wife. They live in Florida. Apparently they were always in love." He shrugged. "It's hard to know what's in someone's heart."

Yeah, he thought, thinking of Kayley.

"Do you ever wonder what your life would

have been like if you hadn't left?" Cade asked as if knowing what his friend was thinking.

Jace scratched at the label on the beer bottle with this thumb for a moment. "I did when I saw Kayley after all these years."

"I really did think the two of you were meant for each other."

Jace took a sip of his beer and said nothing.

"I suppose she told you that she's seeing Ty Reynolds."

Jace's head jerked up.

"I guess she didn't," Cade said. "They've been dating for a while now. I worried she'd just keep carrying a torch for you. I was glad to see her move on."

"She can't be serious about him." The words were out before he could call them back.

Cade laughed. "Spoken like a jealous man. Ty's crazy about her. I wouldn't be surprised if he asked her to marry him at Christmas."

Jace took another drink of his beer, hating the way the news had made his stomach drop. "Ty's a nice guy," he said, making his friend laugh again.

"You really *did* think she was going to wait around for you her whole life."

"No, it's just…" He shook his head, thinking about what a jackass he'd made of himself earlier when he assumed it had been Kayley who'd moved him into his old bedroom. It had probably been some well-meaning friend of Marie's, who was only trying to make him feel more at home. Not Kayley.

What a fool he'd been to think she could still be in love with him after all these years and what he'd done to her.

As he left the bar, he thought about dropping by her house again to apologize but realized it was much too late. No lights were on at her farmhouse as he drove past.

Once in the house, he locked the doors and went up to his room. He thought about moving everything back into the guest room but was too tired and mellow after the beers he'd consumed and spending time with his old friend Cade.

He lay down on his bed, thoughts drifting pleasantly in the past. He woke to the sound of the phone. The clock next to his bed read just a little after midnight. The phone rang three times before Jace could find it.

"Hello."

He could hear someone breathing on the other end of the line.

"Hello?"

A soft click as the person disconnected.

He hung up, thinking nothing of it. Just a wrong number.

Chapter Five

When Kayley opened the door the next morning, she looked wary.

"I'm sorry," Jace said.

She leaned a hip into the door jamb and crossed her arms.

"Someone was in my house. They put my clothes away and left me a present under one of those fake Christmas trees."

"The bastards," she said. "Did they clean, too?"

"I thought—"

"I know what you thought."

"Yeah, well, I'm sorry. I really appreciated you letting me lean on you at the funeral."

"I did that because I knew you didn't have anyone else."

"You felt sorry for me."

She didn't deny it.

"I never deserved you."

She said nothing, those blue eyes of hers simply watching him.

"I guess I've proved once again what a jerk I am. I just wanted to apologize. I won't bother you again." He started to turn away.

"If you're through beating yourself up, would you like a cup of coffee? Unless you think it's part of some evil plot." She held up both hands. "Nothing up my sleeve."

"I'd like that," he said, grinning.

IT WAS THAT GRIN THAT had been responsible for her losing her virginity to him, Kayley thought as she held open the door and Jace stepped in.

That grin, and her love for him. He'd been the love of her life. She'd been so happy when he'd asked her to marry him. Then just weeks later when she'd realized she was pregnant with his baby.

She couldn't help but remember the night she'd told him. Jace had tears in his eyes. She'd never seen him more excited. He was convinced it was a boy. He'd been right about that, she thought at the painful memory of her miscarriage.

As she followed him back to the kitchen, she couldn't help but notice that he'd filled out. He'd left Whitehorse a boy, but he'd come back a strong man. She noticed also that he was wearing cowboy boots again and his old black Stetson. She warned herself that it meant nothing.

She poured him a mug of coffee, and he took a stool at the breakfast bar. She preferred to stand on the other side, cradling her own mug in both hands for the warmth.

Having Jace in this kitchen again was too familiar. They'd spent so many hours here, sitting around talking and laughing. They'd been so close. She'd thought nothing on this earth could come between them.

"How are you doing?" she asked although she knew.

"I've been better."

She could see the sadness in his eyes, the hurt, the regret, the guilt. He hadn't been here when his mother had died. She knew Jace and how that would always haunt him—even if he had a good reason, and she suspected he did.

As hard as he tried not to, he was limping. Something to do with his job, she guessed. All she knew was that it was undercover and dangerous. Marie had worried about him. So had Kayley.

"The place looks the same," he said, glancing around.

"Nothing changes in Whitehorse."

His gaze came back to her as he recognized his own words spoken to her the day he left her. He took a sip of his coffee, eyeing her over the rim of his mug. "Some things change," he said as he put the mug down again. "I heard you're dating Ty."

She nodded, keeping her gaze down.

"I'm happy for you."

Kayley lifted her eyes to his. "Are you?"

"Ty's a nice guy."

She laughed. "You never could stand him, and you know it."

He laughed, too. She'd missed that sound.

"You deserve better."

She shook her head. "If I didn't know you so well, I'd think you were jealous."

He said nothing as he picked up his mug again.

"So, when do you leave?"

His head came up in surprise.

"I know you aren't staying. Whoever put your clothes away doesn't know you as well as I do." Jace had run away twelve years ago. With everything that had happened with his mother and uncle, he must be champing at the bit to get out of here.

"I'm not sure. A couple of days."

She nodded.

"Maybe we could have dinner."

"What did Cade tell you? That I'm serious about Ty? Is that what this is about?"

"*Are* you serious about Ty?"

She turned her back to him to take her mug over to the sink. "You want more coffee?"

"No, thanks. You didn't answer me. Are you going to marry this guy?"

"He hasn't asked me," she said, turning to look at him again.

"So that means you can have dinner with me?"

"I can do whatever I want." She hated that she sounded defensive.

"Good." He grinned. That damned grin of his. "Tonight? Come on, the whole town is already talking since you were by my side at the funeral. What could dinner at the Tin Cup hurt? Unless Ty won't let you go."

Jace was so transparent. He knew she'd

balk at even the suggestion that any man controlled her.

"Great," he said, seeing that he'd won. "I'll pick you up at six." He slid off the stool. "Thanks for the coffee and for forgiving me."

"What makes you think I've forgiven you?"

His gaze locked with hers. How easy it would have been to fall back into those deep, dark eyes. "Maybe someday," he said, regret making his gaze bottomless.

"Maybe." She glanced at her watch. Time to get to work.

And he was gone.

She stood watching him drive away, just as she had twelve years ago. Only back then, she'd believed he would come back for her. Now she was much too smart for that. She'd only agreed to dinner because it had felt like a dare. Proof not only to Jace, but also to herself that she could let him go again.

THE MOMENT JACE WALKED into the house, he'd known someone had been there again. For the past few days his instincts had been so off, he hadn't trusted them.

But his survival skills seemed to be improving, he thought as he checked the front door. No signs of a forced entry, and this time he'd remembered to lock it after finding a set of keys hanging by the back door.

He moved cautiously through the house, doing a thorough search. This time he knew it wasn't Kayley. He'd been a fool to think it had been her the other time. Just the thought of her made him excited about their dinner tonight.

Cade said she'd moved on with Ty Reynolds. After tonight's dinner, Jace thought he'd have a better idea of whether or not that was true.

Not that he wasn't happy for Kayley if it was. He just thought she deserved better than Ty. Kayley needed someone special. He didn't want her to settle. When he was gone from here, he wanted to know that she was truly happy.

As he finished his search of the house, he realized that, just as before, nothing seemed to be missing. Instead, someone had apparently left him another gift.

The bottle of cologne sat on the shelf in his bathroom. He probably wouldn't have noticed it if he hadn't searched the place the day before.

The bottle was new and not a brand he had ever used. He didn't wear cologne, preferring a light aftershave. This cologne was one of those cloying scents he'd always hated.

Why had someone left this for him? And how did they get in?

Grabbing one of the hand towels, he picked up the cologne bottle and carried it downstairs, where he put it in a paper bag.

For a moment he stood in the kitchen, debating what he should do. Was he really going to take this to the sheriff and ask her to check it for fingerprints?

In a few days, he would be gone, so what would be the point? Maybe this was like the shirt, just someone's idea of a thoughtful gift. Or maybe not.

It bothered him since he'd locked the house this time. He wanted to know who'd left it and how they'd gotten in. His gaze took in the kitchen and the mud room beyond it, lighting on a series of small hooks where he'd found the house key hanging. The keys had been clearly marked. Anyone in the house might have seen them and borrowed them long enough to have copies made before replacing them.

Jace picked up the sack with the cologne in it. Now he really did want to know who'd been in the house. He just hoped that whoever had been this brazen hadn't bothered to worry about fingerprints.

AVA HAD KNOWN HER SISTER wouldn't stay away. She just hadn't expected her to come so quickly. Evie was waiting in her motel room when Ava returned from breakfast.

"Evie, I begged you."

"Oh, stop whining." Her sister was sprawled on the bed wearing black leather pants, a red T-shirt and no bra. To make matters worse, she was smoking in Ava's non-smoking room.

"I can't deal with you being here right now," she said. She didn't want Evie to know about Jace. Evie would try to take him away from her, and right now Jace Dennison was the only reason she had to get out of bed in the mornings.

Evie picked up one of the newspapers. "Who is Jace Dennison?"

Her stomach dropped. She'd forgotten all about the newspapers and was now shocked to see that she had circled Jace Dennison's name every time she had found it in an article.

"I met him in the Denver airport. He looks like John," she burst out and had to swallow back that familiar bitter taste of jealousy. "I don't want you around him."

Evie laughed. "Do you think I'll try to take him away from you?"

Ava felt sick. "It wouldn't be the first time." Evie was going to spoil everything.

"You know why you're obsessing over this man?" Evie asked.

"I'm not obsessing."

"It's because you know who he is," she said, lowering her voice.

Ava froze. "What are you saying?"

Evie leaned toward her and whispered, "He's John."

Ava shook her head. "That's crazy."

"Is it? He reminds you of John, doesn't he? I saw the resemblance right away, but it's more than his looks."

"How can it be John?" She wanted desperately for her sister to explain it to her, to give her crazy thoughts and behavior validity.

"Maybe Jace Dennison died, and John's soul was waiting for a body. You don't believe it was a coincidence that you and this man just happened to be in the Denver airport at the same time, do you?"

She didn't, but she didn't dare admit it to her sister. She still wasn't sure if Evie was just fooling with her and would later make fun of her like she used to when they were kids or if Evie suspected what Ava had believed the first time she saw Jace Dennison.

"That sounds crazy," Ava said.

"Maybe not. Didn't I hear that Jace had been in some sort of accident?"

Ava nodded quickly. "His plane crashed. He still has a limp. I saw bandages at his house and a medical report in his bag. He could have been killed."

"You've been to his house?"

She felt tricked. "I was just—"

"So you do believe he is John."

Ava didn't dare voice it.

"If it's John, then on some level he wants you here."

Yes, just as she believed. "You should see the way he looks at me. It's as if he is remembering me, remembering us."

"Ah," Evie said. "It's almost as if you have been given a chance to rewrite history."

Yes. That was exactly it. And also why Ava didn't want her sister anywhere near Jace Dennison.

"Don't look so worried. I wouldn't dream of coming between the two of you. I told you how sorry I was about what happened with me and John."

Ava had to look away. She didn't want her sister to see the doubt in her eyes. She would feel so much better if her sister left town.

As if Evie had heard her, she said, "Maybe I should go to the sheriff."

"Why? I haven't done *anything*." Ava hated how whiny she sounded.

"But you're thinking about doing something."

Was she? Ava moved to the mirror and picked up her hairbrush.

"You can't let what happened to John happen again," Evie said behind her.

Ava looked up to meet her sister's gaze in the mirror.

Her sister just stared back at her, and Ava was suddenly very afraid for Jace Dennison.

TY WAS WAITING FOR HER when Kayley came out of the school. He stood leaning against his pickup.

She felt a stab of guilt—not for accepting Jace's dinner invitation later tonight but for letting her old feelings for him make her completely forget about her lunch plans with Ty. School had been scheduled to let out at 11:30 a.m. today, so she'd made the lunch plans over a week ago.

Ty was a nice guy, and he seemed to care about her, but they only dated on occasion. She was always so busy. That was why Ty had made the lunch date so far in advance.

As she walked over to him, she figured that by now he would have heard that she was with Jace yesterday at the funeral. She wasn't sure what his reaction was going to be.

"Hi," Ty said, shoving back his Western hat to smile at her.

"Hi."

His expression changed instantly. "You forgot about our lunch date," he said, seeing that she had her gym bag.

"I…." She shook her head. "There's just been so much going on."

"Yeah. I would imagine. With Jace being

back in town and the funeral and all. How's he doing?"

She took out her keys and opened her pickup, parked next to his, then dropped her gym bag inside along with her purse. Ty was acting as if it was no big deal, but she heard something in his voice that told a different story.

"Jace is having a hard time, understandably," she said.

Ty nodded. "Understandably. I heard he's put the place up for sale."

That news felt like an ice pick through her heart. Hadn't she known he wouldn't stay? She'd just never imagined he would sell out right away. Was he that anxious to clear out of Whitehorse? Apparently so.

"I'm thinking about making an offer," Ty said. She could feel him watching her closely and knew he'd seen how upset she was. "Apparently he wants out quickly. The place should go for a song."

Kayley didn't blame Ty for rubbing it in. He was angry with her because people were talking about her and Jace being together yesterday at the funeral. She hadn't meant to hurt him. But she had expected more understanding on his part—probably unfairly, since right now her thoughts were more with Jace.

If he was selling the house, that meant he would have no reason to ever come back to Whitehorse. It meant she would never see him again.

Why did that hurt so badly? He'd made it clear twelve years ago that it was over. She hadn't been waiting for him to come back all these years, had she?

The thought made her angry with herself. She knew the score. That was why she'd moved on after years of hardly dating.

"I wouldn't steal it from him," Ty said, no doubt seeing her distress.

"Why would you want it?"

"There's some good pasture along the river. I could rent out the houses to hunters. I've always liked that property."

She suspected he might have another reason for wanting something else that had belonged to Jace.

"I'm sorry about lunch," Kayley said, in no mood to sit through a meal with Ty right now.

"Okay. We can do dinner instead," he said. "Or will you be holding Jace's hand?"

"Ty—"

"I was just kidding, Kayley. I know you were just helping him at the funeral, right?"

"He invited me to dinner tonight. I said I'd go."

Ty was nodding, looking angry, which made her angry with him.

"Jace and I are old friends," she said and regretted that she felt she had to give him a reason.

"*Friends?* He dumped you just weeks before your wedding. He broke your heart. He didn't even come home when the woman who raised him was dying. So please explain what it is you see in him, because it's a damned mystery to me."

She was glad Ty didn't know about the baby she and Jace had lost. But she couldn't explain her relationship with Jace, and even if she could, she didn't want to. "I won't discuss Jace with you. Just because you and I have been dating for a while, Ty—"

"Right," he snapped. "Doesn't mean anything. At least not to you, should your old boyfriend swing back through town. Well, I hope you know what you're doing, sweetheart." She hated it when he called her *sweetheart* in that tone. "Because Jace is going to be gone soon. Gone for good. And where is that going to leave you?"

He turned on his heel, jerked open his pickup door and climbed behind the wheel. A moment later the engine roared and he left, tires throwing gravel as he sped away.

She watched him go, feeling bad. She couldn't really blame Ty. But it was never clearer than at that moment that he wanted more than she could give.

As she got into her own truck, she glanced in the rearview mirror and was startled to see a silver SUV parked down the street. For just an instant, she thought it was Jace sitting behind the wheel.

The vehicle was just like the one Jace was driving. It even had the same rental-car logo on it. No wonder she'd thought it was Jace's.

She realized with a start that it must be the one that had followed her out of town the other day. The same blonde was behind the steering wheel, and Kayley had no doubt she'd been watching her and Ty. As the woman now put up the side window, Kayley realized she'd also probably been listening, as well.

Kayley drove away, watching to see if the woman followed her. She didn't.

JACE FELT LIKE A FOOL as he entered the police department with the cologne in a sack. He was reminded of when he'd come in here two days ago looking for answers, only to get more than a little bad news.

Now he waited for the dispatcher to call the sheriff out.

"Hello, Jace," McCall said.

He felt even more like a fool as he looked at her. Years ago, he should have figured out that they were related. He and McCall Winchester could have passed for brother and sister.

"Someone's been in my house. He or she left this," he said, motioning to the sack he carried. "I'm pretty sure it is just cologne, but I was hoping you could get a print off it. I'd like to know who's fooling with me."

"Step into my office." She led the way down the hall. Once in her office, she placed a call, and a moment later a deputy came to take the sack with the cologne in it. McCall directed the man to see if he could get a print and also to have the lab check the contents.

"Thanks," Jace said, sinking into a chair after the deputy was gone.

"I heard you met my aunt at the funeral."

He nodded. "I saw you at the funeral. Thanks for coming."

McCall smiled, getting his not-so-subtle clue that he didn't want to talk about Virginia Winchester. "Was the cologne the only thing this person left at your house?"

"No, there was a Christmas package with a shirt in it." He hesitated, knowing how crazy it sounded and remembering Kayley's take on it when he'd told her. "The person also put my clothes away in my old room, even though I'd been staying in the guest room."

"Think it might have been a well-meaning neighbor?"

"At first. The cologne threw me. Who buys someone cologne? Not only that—it isn't even something I use."

She nodded. "Once we have the prints, if there are any on the bottle, I'll run them and see what we get. But if it is a neighbor—"

"I know there is little chance of matching any fingerprints." The person would have had to have committed a crime or been fingerprinted for a profession that required it. Like his.

"You want to file a report about the break-in?"

"That's just it—they didn't break in. I think they took the house key off the hook by the back door and possibly made a duplicate."

"You might consider changing the locks."

"I don't plan on being here that long."

"Jace, I know all of this must have you spinning, but I just wanted to let you know. I'm getting married on Christmas out at the ranch. All of the family is invited. That means you're invited."

He drew back, a little surprised. "Thanks. I'd think about it if I was going to be here."

"Well, I just wanted to extend the invitation. You're family if you want to be family, but I understand." She rushed on. "If you'd like to forget that you're related to the Winchesters, I totally understand."

"Yeah, I guess you do," he said with a rueful chuckle. "But you're getting married on the ranch?"

"My grandmother's idea. Our grandmother," she corrected. "Pepper is…"

He raised a brow as she seemed to search for the right word.

McCall laughed. "She's complicated."

"So I've heard." He rose. "Thanks again for the invitation. I hope you have a very happy life."

"Thanks," she said, also rising. "I'm going to try. In the meantime, I'll let you know if we come up with anything on the cologne."

KAYLEY KNEW DINNER WAS a mistake the moment Jace picked her up. It was just like old times. As he held the door open for her at the Tin Cup restaurant, she was reminded of her junior and senior proms. She and Jace had dined here on both occasions.

Both times, Jace had been so handsome and charming that if she hadn't already fallen in love with him, she would have all over again.

He was like that tonight.

"You're awfully quiet," he said after they'd ordered.

"Am I?"

He grinned at her, clearly knowing it was something she couldn't resist.

She tried to relax. "Tell me about your life."

"I can't really—"

"Not the specifics. You travel a lot, right?"

"Yes," he replied wary now.

"Do you have an apartment somewhere?"

"No."

"So you travel light."

"Kayley—"

"I'm just trying to get a picture of what your life is like."

"If you're asking me if I'm sorry that I left—"

"No, I'm not asking that, Jace." Their salads came, and they ate in silence until their entrees arrived.

"So, tell me about *your* life," he said.

She told him about her kindergarten class, some of the funny things the kids said and did, and how exciting it was when she saw how quickly they learned.

"You love your job," he said, sounding surprised. "I didn't know you wanted to be a teacher."

"Neither did I," she said with a laugh. When she and Jace had talked about their future together, it had been a small ranch, with her staying home and raising babies. It amazed her how young they'd been.

"I'm glad things have turned out so well for you," he said, his words belying the sadness she saw in his dark eyes.

"And for you," she said.

After dinner, Jace drove her home, reminiscing about the old days and things they did. At her house, he got out and walked her to the door.

"Thank you for dinner," she said and started to turn to go in, when he grabbed her arm and swung her around. The kiss came as no surprise, but its power was a shocker. Even with strong feelings for Jace, she hadn't expected the passion to still be there. She would have thought the way he'd hurt her, what they'd been through with the baby and the twelve years he'd been gone would have put that fire out.

"Kayley." His voice broke.

"What is it you want, Jace?" she asked on a breath.

He shook his head, looking miserable. A part of her wanted to reach out to him, make it all better, just as she always had.

He leaned toward her, his hat pushed back, that damned grin on his face. "Maybe I missed you."

She shook her head.

"Being with you…"

"You think you might have missed something."

"Think I made a mistake."

She shook her head. "You needed to leave."

"Did I?"

"You must have, because you did."

"I can't help thinking about what might have been. We could have gotten married and had other babies."

"Don't." Kayley reminded herself that Jace had put his property up for sale. He'd feel different in the light of day tomorrow. She'd been here before, and she was too smart to fall again for this man.

That almost made her laugh. She'd never fallen out of love with Jace Dennison. "What do you want, Jace?" she asked again.

He looked into her eyes. "At this moment, there is nothing I want more than you."

She smiled, believing him. "Good night, Jace." As she started to step away, he grabbed her hand and pulled her back to him. They were inches apart, and she knew that if he kissed her again, she would be a goner.

She pulled free and hurried up her porch steps. A part of her half hoped he would follow. At that moment, she wanted him as much as he did her, maybe more.

Once inside, she leaned against the door and listened to him drive away, wondering how many more times she could let him leave her.

JACE MENTALLY KICKED himself all the way home. What had he been thinking, inviting Kayley out to dinner? Hadn't he known it would just remind him of how wonderful things had been between them?

Then he had to go and kiss her?

He hadn't been able to help himself. Kayley had looked so beautiful. Tonight had reminded him why he'd wanted to marry her, why she was still the only woman who could make him feel this way.

Being with her tonight had reminded him of what he'd given up.

His head was spinning. When he thought about it, he was glad that Kayley had sent him packing tonight. He didn't want to hurt her again, and with his life such a mess…

As he locked up, he realized he'd been so involved with the funeral, seeing Kayley again and finding out about his mother and uncle, that he hadn't had time to think about the fact that he was a Winchester.

He wasn't sure how to deal with that—if he had to deal at all. As far as he was concerned, he was Jace Dennison, and once he left White-horse no one would know any different.

But if he decided to stay...

He swore at the thought. Where had that come from?

He found the bottle of whiskey and carried it upstairs. The air temperature felt cooler. He just hoped a winter storm didn't blow in before he left town. He rubbed his leg as he sat down on the bed. It had been aching all day.

The doctor had said he should stay off of it as much as possible until it had a chance to heal. If it didn't heal, he wouldn't be able to go back to work. The thought panicked him. His work was all he'd had for more years than he cared to think about.

All he still had, he reminded himself.

It kept him busy, kept him from thinking...

The realization that he'd spent years fighting to keep Kayley out of his thoughts surprised him. Leaving her had been the hardest thing he'd ever done.

And yet, as she said, he *had* left her.

When he'd left, it had all made sense to

him. He'd really believed he was doing the best thing for both of them.

Seeing Kayley again, though, had him questioning everything—especially why he'd ever left her and why he was trying so hard to get out of town again.

He'd never been a drinker, so it didn't take much before he couldn't keep his eyes open. He lay down on the bed, praying for oblivion.

AVA STOOD STONE STILL, her back against the wall of the guest bedroom next to Jace's room. She'd heard him enter the house and realized how close he'd come to catching her. A few moments later, he had come upstairs, giving her no chance to get away.

She could tell by the sound of his footfalls that his night had not gone well. Her husband, John, used to come home from work like that. His footfalls slow and heavy. She'd be waiting for him with a fresh drink. She loved taking off his shoes and rubbing his feet. She loved the way he looked at her, love in his eyes.

Ava wiped at her sudden tears. John had been the love of her life. Why wouldn't a love like that transcend anything, even death?

In the bedroom next door, she heard Jace Dennison moving around.

Earlier she'd followed him and Kayley Mitchell to the restaurant. She'd watched them through the bank of windows that looked out over the town, trying to gauge what was going on between them. Something, or Jace wouldn't have asked her to dinner.

From the gossip she'd heard this morning at the café, Jace and Kayley were high-school sweethearts—just like her and John. But Jace had left Kayley at the altar—or at least a few weeks before the wedding.

How could a woman forgive a man for something like that? Ava knew she couldn't. But then, John would never have done anything like that to her.

She'd almost gotten caught in the house because she'd thought Jace wouldn't be home until much later. She'd worried he might even spend the night with his old girlfriend, although the thought had hurt her to the core.

"You are such a masochist." She could hear her sister's taunt.

Ava had known coming to the house again was risky, but she hated to keep calling until he answered the phone as she'd done the other night. Anyway, she had a good reason for being here.

Now she listened, heard the creak of the bedsprings and waited. She didn't dare get caught for fear he wouldn't understand.

After twenty minutes passed without a sound, Ava eased open the bedroom door and tiptoed into the hall. The light was off, his door open. Silently, she stepped in.

Chapter Six

Jace woke to bright sunlight streaming into his bedroom window. He blinked, blinded by the light, then saw the bottle of whiskey beside his bed and groaned.

What was he thinking, trying to drink himself into oblivion? It wasn't like him. And yet when things had gotten tough twelve years ago, what had he done? He'd run.

At the memory of last night, he groaned again. Why had he asked Kayley to dinner, let alone kissed her? She'd moved on with Ty Reynolds. She deserved a man she could count on. Maybe Ty was that man.

Sliding his legs over the side of the bed, he sat up. His head ached, and when he reached for his cell phone he saw that he had more messages from his boss.

He didn't have to check them to know his

boss was inquiring as to how the funeral had gone, how his leg was healing, when he'd be back.

Jace rubbed a hand over his face and was just starting to get up to head for the shower when he saw the note. It leaned against the base of the lamp. The handwriting was small, the letters perfectly made.

Jace, My sister is in town. I'm afraid she might hurt you. I'm so sorry, Ava.

Ava? Ava Carris?

His eyes widened. That note hadn't been there last night when he'd gone to bed. He would have noticed it.

Which meant there was only one way that note could have gotten there.

She'd come into his room last night after he'd gone to sleep.

As he rose to snatch up the note, he smelled the faint scent of her perfume and felt his skin go clammy. He read the note again. Her sister? What the hell?

It wasn't until he stood under the hot spray of the shower trying to get his head to clear that Jace realized she must have been the one to leave the present under the tree—and the bottle of cologne.

Hadn't he thought she was stalking him the first time he'd seen her in Whitehorse? He should have followed his own gut instinct.

After toweling dry and dressing, he picked up the note and carefully tucked it into his wallet.

It was time to find Ava Carris and make sure she didn't get into his house again.

But after driving around town, he didn't see her rental SUV at any of the motels or parked in front of Whitehorse's four cafés.

When his cell phone rang, he answered it on the first ring, thinking it would be Ava and that she had gotten his cell-phone number last night when she'd been in his room. Instead, it was the sheriff.

"I ran the prints we found on the bottle of cologne," she said. "Can you stop by?"

"I was already headed there," he said and hung up.

SHERIFF MCCALL WINCHESTER stood as he stepped into her office. "We got a hit on those prints from the cologne bottle," she said after they'd both sat down. "They belong to a woman named Ava Carris."

"Her prints were on file?" He couldn't hide

his surprise. He was sure Ava had left the cologne, but he hadn't expected her prints to be on file.

"You know her?"

"We met at the Denver airport. For whatever reason, I think she followed me to Whitehorse and that she's been stalking me."

McCall raised a brow. "And this is the first you've mentioned it?"

"I really didn't think anything of it. She said I reminded her of her late husband. She seemed confused and lost. I felt sorry for her."

McCall shook her head. "Her prints were on file because she was arrested for killing her husband."

Jace felt his blood turn to ice. How had he gotten the impression that she had adored her husband, was grieving his death? "She *killed* him?"

"According to the evidence."

"Then why isn't she in prison?" he demanded.

"She never stood trial," McCall said. "She was found mentally unable to stand trial and was sent to a psychiatric hospital."

"When was this?" Jace asked, shaken by this news.

"Almost ten years ago."

"What?" He thought he must have heard wrong. When he'd met Ava at the Denver airport he'd gotten the impression she'd only recently lost her husband.

"Ava Carris was released just last week."

Jace was having a hard time taking all this in.

"When I called, you said you were coming to see me," McCall said. "Has something else happened?"

He'd completely forgotten about the note. Digging it out of his wallet, he handed it to her.

McCall read, then looked up at him. "Where did you get this?"

"I found it beside my bed when I woke up this morning."

"She was in your house *again?*" Her tone said he should have taken her advice and changed the locks.

The sheriff read the note again. She looked worried. "I'll see what else I can find out about the murder case and Ava Carris's psychiatric commitment. Maybe there are some conditions to her release—"

"You're telling me you have nothing to charge her on."

"Trespassing. She didn't steal anything. Instead, she left you presents."

"She clearly shouldn't be out on the streets."

"Not according to the medical board in Alaska that released her," McCall said. "I'm not sure what the deal is with her sister, but apparently you look enough like her husband that she might want to harm you and was warning you."

The room suddenly went ice cold. "I have a crazy woman stalking me, and there is nothing I can do about it until she tries to kill me?" Jace raked a hand through his hair and let out a humorless laugh as he put his Stetson back on. "It isn't bad enough that I find out I'm a Winchester—no offense."

"None taken. I should be able to get you a restraining order against her."

A restraining order? She couldn't be serious. "You know how worthless a restraining order is, especially against someone like this."

The irony of it didn't escape him. He made his living protecting other people, and now he was the one who needed the protection.

"You could always go stay at the Winchester ranch. She'd have a hard time finding you there."

He shoved to his feet. "That's like telling me to jump out of the frying pan into the fire to save myself. No thanks."

"Then at least get the locks changed on the house."

He knew the best thing he could do was to get out of Dodge as quickly as possible. Let Ava Carris or her sister try to find him after he left here.

In the meantime, if he and Ava crossed paths again, he'd have to handle it himself.

KAYLEE HADN'T SLEPT WELL after her dinner with Jace. The kiss had rattled her more than she wanted to admit. She still loved him. She'd never stopped loving him and doubted she ever would.

But where did that leave her?

She'd lain in bed into the wee hours of morning considering just that. Did she really believe there was only one person on this earth for her? Maybe that wasn't true for everyone, but she knew it was for her.

She'd called Ty first thing to tell him she

was sorry but that she wouldn't be seeing him anymore.

"You and Jace aren't getting back together," he'd said, but without as much conviction as yesterday.

"No. But I will always love him, and it isn't fair to you. You deserve someone who loves you with all her heart."

Kayley had just hung up when her phone rang. It was her good friend Shawna. "Ty just called me. He said you've lost your mind."

She had to laugh both because she probably had lost her mind and because it was just like Ty to run to her friend. Now that she thought of it, Ty and Shawna had a lot more in common than she and Ty did.

"He says you broke up with him because of Jace? Kayley—"

"I didn't *break up* with him. We were never more than friends."

"He's a nice guy."

If Kayley had a nickel for every time someone had said that to her… "He's not the man for me."

Shawna sighed. "Sweetie, Ty says that Jace is selling his place. He isn't sticking around."

"I know."

"But this is about Jace, isn't it."

It was. "It's hard to explain, and I haven't the time to try right now. I have to get to school," she said and hung up.

Now, as she looked over the young heads of her busy students, she couldn't help but let herself think about Jace and the future. What did she want? She'd asked Jace what he wanted last night, but she'd never really considered what she wanted.

She glanced toward the window and was startled to see a silver SUV parked outside. For just a split second, she thought the driver behind the wheels was Jace. But then she saw that it was that woman again.

Rising from her desk, she moved to the window, unable to shake off the chill that ran the length of her spine. The woman, having seen her, started her vehicle and quickly drove off. But Kayley felt unsettled the rest of the school day.

THE CALL CAME OUT OF the blue.

"I have an offer on your place," Jace's real estate agent told him.

He hadn't expected this. He'd figured it

would take months and that he would be doing the paperwork by fax and email.

When Clare told him for how much, he'd been surprised. He'd convinced himself he was willing to settle for a lot less just to get out of town. But that had been a few days ago.

"So, how long does all this take?" he asked, suddenly feeling rushed.

"If you accept the offer, I can push it through in the next few days. The buyer offered to wave a lot of the conditions that take time, like having the property surveyed and requiring a list of the farm and ranch equipment. He's even offered to buy what livestock you have."

Wow, Jace thought. It sounded as if the buyer wanted him out of town as much as he wanted to leave.

"Who is this buyer?" he asked.

Clare was silent for a moment. "I'm sure you'll hear around town anyway. Ty Reynolds."

Ty? Jace shook his head. He should have known. "Maybe we should wait. If someone jumped on it this quickly, maybe I should hold out for more money," he said, only half joking.

"I thought you were in a hurry and would take even less to get it settled."

He had thought so, too. Maybe it was just the thought of Ty Reynolds owning his place. He knew he was being foolish. Did he really give a damn who owned the place once he was out of here?

"Send me the offer, and I'll look it over."

"I would advise you to definitely consider it. This offer is more than what acreage is going for right now, and with him willing to wave some of the conditions that usually hold up a sale..."

"Yeah, I'm sure you're right." He took a breath and let it out. Ty was going to have not only the house he'd grown up in, but also his property—and Kayley. "Let's just get it over with. I'll stop by and sign the papers."

"Tomorrow afternoon, say, two?"

"Great." He hung up and swore. With the property sold there would be nothing keeping him in Whitehorse. Wasn't this what he'd wanted?

Jace recalled Kayley asking what he wanted last night. He'd wanted her. Now he stepped out on the front porch. She would be home from teaching school by now. If he climbed up on the porch railing, he could just make out Kayley's house in the distance. He'd forgotten that he used to do that all the time when he was a teenager. He and Kayley had a sign back then…

He looked at the window that used to be her bedroom. She would hang a flag in the window to let him know what was going on.

Instead, now, he saw Ty Reynolds's pickup was parked out front.

TY FELT BAD ABOUT HIS argument with Kayley. He felt even worse about her phone call this morning. But now that he was here in her house, he felt his original anger begin to surface again.

Nothing had gone as he'd planned it from the moment Jace Dennison had returned to town, and matters hadn't improved since he'd showed up unannounced on Kayley's doorstep. Clearly, she hadn't been happy to see him.

He'd even had to invite himself inside. She hadn't offered him anything to drink, which wasn't like her. He could smell hot apple cider cooking on the stove, and yet she'd led him into the living room, where they both now sat.

"Look, I'm sorry about some of the things

I said yesterday in the school parking lot," he said. "I care about you. I just don't want to see you get hurt."

Her smile never reached her eyes. "I appreciate that, Ty, but I really can take care of myself."

"I'm not sure that's true when it comes to Jace Dennison," he said, feeling his anger rise even more. "Sorry, but so far you've behaved like a doormat when it comes to him. Do you really think it was your place to be at his side at the funeral? I mean, everyone in town is talking."

Kayley was on her feet, and he knew he'd overstepped again.

"Please," he said, holding up both hands and staying seated. He wasn't leaving until he'd said what he'd come to say. "What I'm saying is—"

"I know what you're saying. That's why I'd like you to leave. It's really none of your business."

That hit him like a punch. He looked up at her, unable to believe she'd just said that. "None of my business?"

"Ty, I've enjoyed your company for the past few months...."

"We've been dating for over a year." He bit off each word.

"But we're just friends. You knew that from the start."

He laughed, remembering the times he'd tried to take their relationship to the next level and she'd held him off—literally. "I thought in time—"

"I've been clear about my feelings. I'm sorry you wanted more. I think you're right. We shouldn't see each other anymore."

Now he was on his feet. Had he said he didn't want to see her anymore? She was putting words into his mouth, damn her. "Kayley, you're being irrational."

The moment the words were of his mouth and he saw her expression, he knew he'd blown it.

"I really would appreciate it if you would leave before I become more irrational and do something you will regret."

"I didn't mean to say that. What I meant was—"

But she had already left the room and was now waiting for him, holding the door open.

He could see that there was nothing to say that would change her mind—at least not at this moment. He told himself that once Jace Dennison was gone, she would change her mind.

Hat in hand, he left, wincing as she slammed the door behind him.

VIRGINIA PULLED DOWN the road, almost losing her nerve when she saw the vehicle parked in front of the house and realized that Jace was home.

She parked and sat for a moment, half hoping he would come out and run her off. Better than going to the door and having him turn her away.

Getting out, she looked around the ranch. It didn't compare to the Winchester ranch in any way, but then few ranches did. But this was where her son had grown up. Just miles from the Winchester ranch. Not that she had been around to see him grow up the past twenty-seven years, she reminded herself.

Her mother had run her children off twenty-seven years ago after losing her youngest son, Trace. A recluse all those years until recently, Pepper would never be nominated for mother of the year.

As Virginia walked toward the front door,

she wondered what kind of mother she would have been. She'd never had a chance to find out, but if there was even a chance she would have been like her mother, she was glad Marie Dennison had raised Jace instead of her.

She knocked, then stood looking around. It was getting dark. She should have stopped by earlier, but it had taken a while to get up her courage.

Once she'd heard that Jace had put the place up for sale, she'd known that if she wanted to talk to her son, it wasn't something she could put off. She'd worried that she'd never forgive herself if she didn't make the effort.

She started to knock again, when the door opened and there he was, in a T-shirt and jeans. He was barefoot, and his dark hair, so like her own, was still wet from the shower.

"I hope I didn't catch you at a bad time," she said, sounding like a door-to-door saleswoman. "I was hoping we could talk."

She saw him hesitate. He looked as if he'd rather have a root canal, but he opened the door wider and motioned her in.

"Would you like—" he paused as if thinking better of whatever he'd been about to ask, then continued "—to sit down." He motioned toward the small living room.

"Thank you." She sat down on the edge of the couch.

"So, what is it that you want?" he asked without sitting down.

She looked around without answering. With obvious reluctance, he sat down across from her.

"I wanted to meet you," Virginia said, trying not to stare at him.

"We met at the funeral."

She nodded. "You are so handsome."

He looked uncomfortable.

"This is as strange to me as it is to you."

"I doubt that," he said.

"I have a grown son that I'd never seen until yesterday. That is pretty strange."

"I'm not your son. Not in a way that matters."

She nodded. "I can understand you feeling that way. But I loved your father, and he loved me."

"Then why weren't the two of you married?"

"It's complicated."

Jace shook his head. "Your lover's mother

paid someone to switch the babies. Sounds pretty simple to me. I think I lucked out."

The words hurt because she agreed with him. "I think you did, too."

"Look, we really have nothing to say to each other," he said, getting to his feet. "I don't mean to be rude…"

"No, I understand," she said, rising, as well. "I'm sorry that you had to find out. I would never have told you if it had been up to me. The last thing I wanted was for you to be upset by this."

He let out a bark of a laugh. "Upset? Upset is when you can't find your keys. Upset isn't finding out that your uncle was a murderer and that you are the spawn of the most notorious family in town. Trust me, I'm a hell of a long way past upset, and I can't wait until I can put this dusty wide spot in the road behind me."

She nodded. "Thank you."

"Why would you thank me?"

"You let me in the door," she said with a rueful smile. "I hadn't even expected that. I can see myself out."

And with that she left. It wasn't until she was a couple miles down the road that she had to pull over because she was crying so hard she could no longer see the road.

JACE PACED THE FLOOR after Virginia Winchester left. He was angry at her for coming to his house and even angrier at himself for the way he'd treated her. But she'd ambushed him. If she'd called…

If she'd called, he would have told her to stay away.

He knew his mother…. Marie would have been disappointed in him. He was disappointed in himself. But Virginia Winchester had caught him off guard, and he'd taken his anger out on her.

Snatching up his keys, he headed out the door, not knowing where he was going. He was just too worked up to sit around the house.

His vehicle took him straight to Kayley's. Even as he pulled into the yard, he was telling himself to turn around. He had no business here, even if Ty's pickup was gone.

As he started to turn around, the porch light came on and she appeared in the doorway.

Just the sight of her made him bring the SUV to a stop. He sat for a moment before he cut the engine and climbed out.

"I don't know what I'm doing here," he said at the bottom of her porch steps.

"I guess you'd better come in where it's warm and figure it out," she said.

"Kayley—"

"It's cold out, Jace. Unless you're afraid I'm going to work my womanly wiles on you, then I suggest we do this inside."

She turned and walked back into the house, leaving the door open. He climbed the steps, telling himself with each one that this was a mistake.

The house smelled of ginger cookies. He followed the familiar scent into the kitchen, where Kayley was making gingerbread men. Her mother always made them for the Christmas tree. But Kayley didn't have a tree yet.

She wore a faded apron that he knew had been her mother's, but even so she had flour on her jeans and a smudge on her cheek. Her blond hair was pulled back, making her cheekbones seem more prominent and her eyes more wide and innocent.

"You can have a cookie," she said. "But take one of the ones I messed up. They're for my kindergarten class."

The smell transported him back to other

Christmases when it would have been her mother making the cookies and him and Kayley sitting at the breakfast bar eating the ones that weren't perfect.

"You can help me decorate them while we figure out what brought you here," she said, pushing a small bowl of raisins toward him. "You do remember how to do this, don't you?"

How to be in the same room with her without kissing her? Or putting raisin eyes on gingerbread men?

"I remember." He watched her make a line of white icing piping around the edge of a cookie, then two dots for the eyes before passing it to him for the raisins.

"My birth mother came by to see me," he said as he reached for two more raisins.

Kayley didn't look up from icing a cookie. "That must have been hard for her." So like Kayley to think of the other person.

"I was rude to her."

She looked up at him then.

"This whole thing has just thrown me. I hate the way I'm handling everything."

"Well, you don't have much longer. Once you leave here—"

"It's not that easy." He was searching her face. "I'm sorry I hurt you. First my dad, then our baby…"

She started to continue icing the cookie, but he reached out and stilled her hand.

"I know I took the easy way out by running, Kayley. But suddenly it was as if the walls were caving in on me…."

She tried to pull free, but he held on until he saw that the icing had dripped onto the cookie, making a pool of white.

He let go, saw her look down, her eyes filling with tears. He was on his feet and around the breakfast bar in an instant.

Carefully he took the tube of icing from her and laid it down on the counter before he pulled her to him.

"The cookies—"

"Kayley." He looked into her eyes and felt as if he'd really come home. He hadn't planned to kiss her again. Hell, he hadn't planned to even come over here.

She came to him as he pulled her closer, her lips parting as if she'd known all along it was only a matter of time until he kissed her.

When he drew back, he said, "Kayley, I—"

But she stopped him with a finger on his lips and quickly replaced it with her mouth.

His arms around her, he grabbed a handful of her shirt in both hands and pressed her back against the opposite counter, losing himself in her.

A part of him knew he should stop, but he felt incapable as she unsnapped his Western shirt and pressed her palms against his chest, a moan escaping her lips.

His mouth slipped from hers to drop down the slim column of her neck to the open collar of her shirt. Damn, how he'd missed the smell of her, the taste of her.

He fumbled at the buttons for a moment before she moved his hands aside and unbuttoned her shirt. He trailed kisses across the rounded tops of her full breasts, peeling back the lacy bra to ferret out her rock-hard nipple.

She arched against him as he cupped her waist in his two hands and lifted her up onto the kitchen counter, his tongue teasing her hard nipple as his hands worked at the buttons of her jeans. When he had them open, he snaked a hand into her lacy underpants and touched her warm, wet center.

His gaze met hers, and desire sparked between them like a jolt of electricity between two live wires. Sliding her off the counter and into his arms, he carried her to her bedroom.

When he laid her on the bed, she pulled him down beside her, working to get his jeans off. He let out a moan of pleasure as he stripped away the last of her clothes. Finally, melded by the heat of their naked skin, they rocked together, making the bed squeak and groan just as it had so many years ago when they'd promised to love each other forever.

FROM WHERE HE WAS PARKED in a grove of trees nearby, Ty stared at Kayley's house, willing Jace Dennison to leave.

He glanced at his watch and felt his ire rise. When was the bastard going to leave? Kayley's bedroom light had gone off a good twenty minutes ago.

Ty had felt sick when he'd seen the light come on behind the curtains in her bedroom. He'd thought about storming up to the house and pounding on the door and making a complete jackass of himself.

Hadn't he known she would fall right back in Jace's arms? Did she really think this changed anything? She was so naive. Now he would have to pick up the pieces when Jace broke her heart.

He'd wanted Kayley since high school, but she'd been Jace Dennison's. When Jace had dumped her just weeks before their wedding, Ty had thought he stood a chance.

But he'd found himself waiting patiently for her to go to college and come back. He'd known she would, and he'd been right. It had seemed like fate.

He'd known that Jace came back occasionally but sneaked into town and out without seeing anyone.

He'd always wondered if Kayley had known Jace was in town. But she'd never let on, so he'd assured himself that she was over Jace Dennison.

Now he saw how foolish that had been on his part. Jace shows up and crooks a finger at her and she goes running.

He was furious with her and told himself that after Jace left he'd let her hang for a while. Let her wonder if he would ever forgive her.

Meanwhile, he had to get Jace out of town. The longer he stayed, the more angry Ty was becoming.

He reached for the key in the ignition, just wanting to get out of there. He'd gotten much more than he'd come for.

But before he could start his car, a dim light flashed on in the woods across the road from his hiding place. He realized with a start that it was another vehicle and the light he'd seen was the dome light coming on for an instant. He wouldn't have seen it except that the driver was now pulling out, leaving just like he was with his lights off.

Was it just some teenagers parking and making out in the trees? Odd place to do it.

As the SUV started to pull away, he hit his headlights. The driver looked startled, turning in his direction, clearly as unaware as Ty had been that he wasn't alone out here hiding in the trees.

He was almost as startled when he saw that it wasn't a man behind the wheel but a woman. No one else in the car. No teenagers making out in the trees.

As she sped off toward town, Ty wondered what the woman had been doing out here hiding in the trees all alone.

With a chill he realized she had to have

been watching Kayley's house—just as he had been.

Ty reached for his phone, thinking he needed to call Kayley and warn her. But he quickly put his cell phone away. The only way to warn her would be to admit what he'd been doing out here in the dark.

Anyway, what was the big deal about some woman watching Kayley's house? Must be some woman interested in Jace. What else could it be?

Chapter Seven

When she woke later that night, Kayley lay on her side, leaning on one elbow and staring into Jace's handsome sleeping face. She was trying to memorize everything about him. She knew this changed nothing. Well, at least for Jace.

He looked so relaxed she had to smile. She had known he would come to her. She'd been waiting. And ever since his return, she'd been asking herself what it was that she wanted.

She wanted this last night with him. It was selfish and probably foolish, but she didn't care. She knew the score. They had no future, and she had finally accepted that.

So, yes, she'd known this was where they would end up. She felt a little guilty because clearly Jace hadn't known they would end up making love. She touched her stomach, placing her hand over it. Jace had just assumed she was on the pill, just assumed she was sleeping with Ty. He should have known her better.

Tears brimmed in her eyes at the thought that she might have conceived Jace's baby. It was what she wanted, what she had decided. She told herself Jace would never know. He was selling out here, leaving for good. All she wanted was just a little of him for herself.

As she looked into his handsome face, she didn't ask herself if that was fair. Life wasn't fair.

Jace would leave tomorrow just as he had planned. He would run, just as he had twelve years ago. He was scared of loving too much. She understood that. They each had to deal with that on their own terms.

She knew he would awaken with regrets. She didn't want him to feel badly. Or to think that this changed anything. The one thing she had to be was strong enough to let him go.

Kayley carefully climbed out of bed, not wanting to wake him and picked up her clothes to carry down the hall to dress. It was one thing to know that he would regret what they'd done. She couldn't bear to see it in his dark eyes the moment they opened.

Worse, that he would feel he had to apologize.

That was why he could never know about the baby—if she was lucky enough to conceive.

Going back into the kitchen, she put her apron on and began to decorate the cookies for her class. She knew she could raise a baby. She had a good job, a house and lots of friends and extended family who would be there for her. It was too bad Jace wouldn't be a part of it, but he'd made his choice and so had she.

As she worked finishing the cookies, she thought about making love with him and smiled even as she fought back tears. It had always been amazing. She knew no other man would ever compare. Nor could she love anyone the way she loved Jace—except for his child.

JACE WOKE AND FOR A moment couldn't remember where he was. Kayley. The lovemaking came back in a heated rush. He lay back furious with himself for coming here and at the same time unable to regret being with her again.

He just didn't want to hurt her, and he knew that in his state of mind he'd had no business coming to her. He could hear her in the kitchen as he rose and pulled on his clothes. Why hadn't she thrown him out on his ear? What was wrong with this woman?

As he opened the bedroom door, he heard her singing along with a Christmas carol on the radio. He found her icing the cookies, just as she had been when he'd arrived.

He stood for a moment just watching her, wishing… Hell, what was he wishing? He shook his head, telling himself he needed to get out of this town before he hurt her any more than he already had.

"Hey," she said as if sensing him standing there. "You have to eat the one you made me mess up."

He moved to the counter and picked up the gingerbread man covered with a thin sheen of white icing and took a bite. He couldn't remember the last time he'd eaten, but instantly he remembered the taste of these cookies in this house.

"These are even better than the ones your mother made," he said.

"Flatterer," she said but didn't look at him.

"Kayley, about earlier—"

"Hand me the raisins," she said.

He did. "I just want to say—"

"I was thinking," she interrupted again. "I

could have a garage sale for you, if you'd like. My class is always looking for fund-raisers. I know you won't want to keep any of the furniture in the house. I imagine the only thing you'll want are your father's guns."

She looked up then, and he was struck once again by how well she knew him. He'd already put his father's guns away for safekeeping the last time he was in town—except for a handgun he kept at the house that his mother had used to scare away skunks and coyotes.

"Sure," he said, "help yourself." He couldn't believe this is what she wanted to talk about after what had happened upstairs. "You're welcome to anything you want."

"Thanks." She finished putting the last of the eyes on the cookies then dusted her hands on her apron. "I didn't realize it was so late," she said pointedly.

He cocked a brow. She was throwing him out?

"If I don't see you again before you leave, take care of yourself," she said, stepping to him to plant a kiss on his cheek.

He reached for her, wanting to hold her in his arms once more, but she quickly stepped back. "You, too," he said and let her walk him to the door. "Kayley," he tried explaining again out on the dark porch.

"Goodbye, Jace," she said and closed the door behind him.

He stood on the step, feeling as if she'd slammed the door on him. Things felt unfinished, but clearly not for Kayley. He swore, realizing that leaving her this time was even more painful than the last.

As he drove down her road toward the highway, he told himself that after he was gone she'd marry Ty and live happily ever after.

Somehow that didn't make him feel any better.

AFTER A FITFUL NIGHT, Jace woke with a raging headache. He knew he'd messed up going to Kayley's last night. He hadn't thought about the consequences. He hadn't cared. He'd needed her, desperately wanted her. No wonder she'd thrown him out afterward.

He couldn't blame her. She knew he hadn't changed his mind about leaving. What she didn't know was how much last night with her had affected him. He had lain in bed questioning the decision he'd made twelve years ago, questioning what he was doing with his life, questioning why he had never been able to forget Kayley—even as hard as he'd tried.

In the wee hours of the morning, he'd finally fallen asleep after barring the doors and slipping his father's pistol under his pillow. But it hadn't been Ava Carris who'd filled his dreams. It had been Kayley.

When the phone rang late the next morning, he'd hoped it was her. But he remembered the way she'd said goodbye last night, closing the door on the two of them for good. He didn't think she could be much clearer.

It, of course, wasn't Kayley but Cade calling to invite him to dinner.

He jumped at it, glad that Cade had called. "Great. See you about six then."

He'd fallen back asleep, surprised how exhausted he was from everything that had been going on. At least that's what he told himself later when he woke late in the afternoon.

After showering, he wandered downstairs, looking through the house, thinking about what Kayley had said about selling everything for him. Wasn't there something he wanted to keep?

He brushed his fingers over his mother's knickknacks, thought of his great-grandmother's china used only for special occasions and pulled out the photo albums. Sitting down, he began to go through the snap-shots of him as a baby with his mother and father and Uncle Audie.

His mother had been religiously prompt at getting the photographs into albums. There were dozens of albums. He slowed as he pulled out one that was filled with snapshots of him and Kayley. Had they ever been that young?

Laughing, he touched his finger to a photo of him and Kayley when they were about nine. They were both dressed in their best Western attire, on the way to a rodeo, as he recalled. They were smiling at the camera, but their eyes were cut toward each other. Had they known even then that they would always love each other?

Seeing the clock and realizing he was late, Jace quickly put the albums back and got ready to go to dinner. As he drove past Kayley's he was more pleased than he should have been to see that Ty's pickup wasn't parked out front.

On the way through town, he drove past the row of motels. No sign of Ava's rented SUV. He breathed a sigh of relief. He had enough on his mind without a crazy woman stalking him.

Cade and Andi lived in a new house he'd built south of Nelson Reservoir. Jace saw the horse barn before anything else. It was huge. Cade had always loved raising horses. Apparently he'd made quite a business out of it.

Jace was happy for his friend as he turned into the drive and saw the beautiful home he'd built. The design had stayed true to Montana and was rustic on the outside.

He and Kayley could have had a place like this, he thought. The thought made his heartache. He'd burned that bridge repeatedly. Even if he changed his mind about everything, he doubted Kayley would ever trust him. She'd asked him what he'd wanted. He thought he'd known. Now, though...

The inside of the house reflected the Jacksons' lifestyle. Andi welcomed him warmly and took his coat, inviting him into the kitchen, where Cade was barbecuing on an indoor grill. He handed Jace a beer and told him to pull up a stool.

"I didn't know you could cook."

His friend laughed. "Andi taught me. Now everything I cook is Tex-Mex."

His wife elbowed him good-naturedly in the ribs. "He's exaggerating, although we do eat our share of peppers and tortillas."

The kitchen was warm, painted in yellows and reds. Jace breathed in the wonderful scents coming from the grill and the oven and felt a stab of envy to see how happy his friend was. If he hadn't known better, he'd have thought Cade had just invited him over to show him what he was missing.

Just then the front door opened. He felt a gust of cool fall air and an instant later caught Kayley's wonderful scent as she came into the kitchen.

Her arms were full. Andi greeted her, taking the bouquet of flowers and a pan of what looked like chocolate cake from her.

Jace suspected it was his favorite cake. But when Kayley saw him, there was no mistaking her shocked expression. She looked uncomfortable, then narrowed her eyes at Andi, who gave her a grin and a shrug.

"Kayley," Jace said, moving over a stool so she could join him.

She hesitated only a moment before she slid upon a stool next to him. Cade offered her a beer. She took a long pull on it, as if she needed the diversion.

"Honey, can you help me for a moment?" Andi said and motioned Cade into the other room.

He turned down the grill, promising to be right back, and followed his wife.

"I think we've been set up," Jace said.

"It certainly appears that way," Kayley said, not looking at him.

"I suppose we should make the best of it."

"I suppose." She finally looked over at him. He met her blue gaze.

"Here's to well-meaning friends," he said and raised his beer bottle.

She smiled. "Friends." And touched her bottle to his.

Cade and Andi returned, Cade at least looking a little sheepish.

Dinner was filled with good food, laughter and lots of conversation. Jace couldn't remember a dinner he'd enjoyed more.

Kayley seemed so at ease in their company, making him realize this wasn't her first time in the Jackson home. He felt a strange sense of jealousy. Kayley really had gotten on with her life. Jace felt as if he was still where he'd been twelve years ago.

After dinner, Cade took him out to see his new horses. "You okay, old buddy?"

"It's so strange being back here," Jace said.

"Thanks," his friend joked.

"No, seriously, I feel so out of it—as if I've never belonged here. Other times it feels as if I've never left."

"And that's a bad thing?"

"No, that's just it. That's what's so strange. It isn't bad. I find myself wishing I never *had* left."

Cade lifted an eyebrow. "But you did leave, and from what I hear, plan on leaving again as soon as possible."

"When I first got back, all I could think about was getting out of here. Everything felt as if it was closing in on me."

"It was a lot to come home to," Cade agreed. "Has something changed?"

Jace shrugged. "I find myself questioning why I left here."

His friend stopped to study him. "You sure it isn't just being around Kayley again? By the way, tonight was Andi's doing, not mine."

"Kayley is part of it, I'll admit. But it's more than that. I've missed having a friend like you. In my line of work, you don't get too attached to anyone, any place, anything."

"I can't imagine living like that," Cade said.

"It was what I thought I wanted and needed. But now…" He shook his head.

"What would you do if you stayed?"

"Ranch." The word was out, surprising him since he hadn't given it a thought.

"You sure this isn't just a case of nostalgia and in a few days you're going to wish you were out of here?" Cade sounded worried.

Jace hadn't expected his friend to take this attitude. "I thought you'd be excited about the prospect of my staying."

"I would be if it is for the right reasons."

"And what would those be?" Jace demanded.

"I don't know. Do you?"

Jace swore. "You're afraid I'm going to hurt Kayley again."

"Aren't you?"

He wanted to deny it, but look what he'd done just last night. "Thanks for dinner, the beer and the advice." He turned and went back to the house.

Andi and Kayley were talking in the living room in front of the fireplace when he walked in.

"Thanks for a wonderful dinner," he told Andi. "Kayley, it was great to see you again, but I should get going."

Kayley didn't look surprised that he was leaving.

He tipped his hat and left, hating that Cade might be right.

CADE CAME BACK IN THE house just minutes after Jace had driven away.

Kayley knew the two of them had gotten into some sort of argument from just the way Jace had acted and the look on Cade's face.

"Cade," Andi said, dragging out the word. "What did you do?"

"Nothing," he said holding up both hands. "I just had a talk with him."

Both Kayley and Andi groaned.

"Someone had to do it," Cade said, glancing at Kayley.

"I'm a big girl, Cade. I can take care of myself," she said, getting to her feet. "But I do appreciate the thought," she added with a smile.

Cade had always been like a big brother to her. She couldn't be happier for him since he and Andi had gotten together. He'd been through a lot with his first wife dying in a car accident on the day they'd found out she was pregnant with his child.

Andi had told her tonight that she was expecting. She and Cade had decided not to say anything until now. They'd gotten married last summer south of Old Town Whitehorse at the home of Cade's brother Carter and sister-in-law, Eve.

There'd been a rash of babies in Whitehorse. Kayley had felt a tug at her heart when Andi had told her.

"I should go, too. Thank you so much for inviting me."

"Really?" Andi said sheepishly.

"Really." She hugged Andi and Cade and, taking her cake pan, left. She fought tears as she drove home. Jace had been his old self at dinner, charming, relaxed, funny and fun. He'd made her miss him all the more.

At first she'd been upset with her friend for setting her up. But later she'd thanked her.

Kayley would have given anything for this evening with her friends and Jace.

Nothing could spoil it, she thought as she turned down the lane toward home. Not even Jace leaving so abruptly—or Ty's pickup parked in front of her house.

JACE STOPPED ON HIS WAY through White-horse at the Mint Bar. He didn't so much want a drink as he didn't want to go back to that empty house with just him and his thoughts.

He was nursing a beer when he happened to look in the mirror behind the bar and saw her.

Ava Carris was sitting in a booth in the shadowy darkness behind him.

It gave him a start. He'd been so sure she'd left town. Wrong.

Had she been sitting in that booth when he'd come in? No. That meant she must have followed him. Had she followed him all day?

He couldn't be sure. His mind had been on Kayley. He hadn't even thought to check for a tail. In his line of work it would have been second nature. Just not here in Whitehorse, where he'd felt safe.

With a curse, he told himself this had to

stop. Taking his beer, he stepped over to her table.

As he approached, she smiled broadly. She looked different, and he realized she wasn't wearing her usual conservative slacks, top and matching jacket with sensible shoes. A woman who definitely hadn't looked like a crazed murderer.

Now, though, she was wearing jeans, a T-shirt and boots. She wore more makeup, and even her hair was a little different. He realized he was getting a glimpse of another Ava.

"You have to quit following me," he said, in no mood to mince words.

She cocked her head at him coyly. "Why don't you sit down, handsome, and we can talk about it?"

"I'm serious. I don't want to see you get in trouble again, Ava."

She laughed and slid over in the booth. "Call me Eva." She patted the seat next to her. "You and I have more in common than you might think."

"You have me confused with your husband."

Her eyebrow shot up. "Not hardly. John was as dull as dirt." She laughed, a low laugh that sent a chill through him. "I have a feeling you're a lot more fun."

"Stop. Following. Me. Or I will have to go to the sheriff."

"You aren't really going to have me arrested?"

He could see that she wasn't the least bit worried about the sheriff.

"I'm warning you," he said and put down his half-full beer. He'd lost all desire for a beer— or this bar. "You don't realize who you're dealing with."

He turned to leave.

"Wait." As he turned back, her entire expression had changed. She looked more like she had the first time he'd seen her. She looked around as if confused, then flushed, tears welling in her eyes.

"I'm so embarrassed." She reached for the paper cocktail napkin beneath her drink to wipe at her eyes. "I'm sorry. I don't know what is wrong with me."

He suspected he did, though. "Do you have someone you can talk to?"

Her eyes widened. "You mean like a psychiatrist?"

"Or a friend." He'd almost said relative, but

remembered the note she'd left by his bed. He wasn't about to suggest her sister.

"I just get confused sometimes, that's all. I have a number to call when I'm feeling…upset. You don't have to worry about me anymore. I'm leaving Whitehorse tomorrow. Please forgive me for my behavior. I'm having a difficult time readjusting to life." She dropped her head. "I've been…away."

He didn't know what to say. He felt sorry for her and, at the same time, afraid for her. She seemed so fragile, so close to the edge.

"Take care of yourself," he said.

She looked up and smiled through her tears. "Thank you. You, too."

As he left the bar, he couldn't shake off the feeling that Ava Carris had just warned him again.

"FUN NIGHT?" TY ASKED as Kayley got out of her pickup. He was sitting in the dark at the edge of her porch but now stepped out where she could see him.

Not that she needed to see him to know he was angry. Had he heard about her dinner with Andi and Cade? But how could he have known

Jace was going to be there, since she hadn't known herself?

"What do you want, Ty?" she asked as she went up the steps and opened her front door. The house wasn't locked. She was thankful he hadn't let himself in.

He followed her into the kitchen now, glancing at the three pieces of chocolate cake left in the pan. Kayley had tried to get Andi to keep it, but her friend had said that now that she was pregnant, she would know it was down in the kitchen and get up in the middle of the night and eat all three pieces.

Kayley thought about offering Ty a piece of cake, but caught herself. She sensed he'd been drinking, and that only added to his foul mood. Better to keep this short.

Also, it was Jace's favorite cake. She'd been embarrassed that she'd made it. But she'd been thinking about him, and when Andi had asked her to bring dessert, she'd felt like baking it.

"I need to know where we stand," Ty said, pulling out a stool at the breakfast bar.

"It's late," she said, wondering if it was smart to get into this tonight the way she was feeling. She'd already told him where they stood. Nowhere.

"Too late for you and me?"

The change in his tone from angry to sad made her soften her words.

"Ty, we've talked about this. I can't keep seeing you."

"It's Jace, isn't it?"

She said nothing into the silence that followed. "You knew what the score was going in."

"Yeah," he said, pushing himself to his feet. "I knew. But I guess I just kept hoping you'd come to your senses."

"I really don't think we should talk about this tonight."

"You were with Jace, weren't you." He swore. "Don't bother to deny it. I can tell by the way you're acting. Don't you see what he does to you? The sad thing is that he is going to break your heart all over again. How long are you going to carry a torch for a man who doesn't want you?"

"I think you should leave."

Ty shoved the stool out of his way. It toppled to the floor, hitting with a loud crack as he stormed out. A moment later the front door slammed.

Kayley stood listening until she heard his

pickup engine rev, the sound dying off down the road. Then she picked up the stool and sat down on it to have a piece of cake before turning in.

JACE CALLED THE SHERIFF on his way home. He got one of her deputies who promised to swing by the Mint Bar and talk to Ava. It wouldn't hurt, Jace figured. Maybe it would just get her out of town a little sooner.

Unlocking the door, he stepped inside and headed for the kitchen. He found the quart of orange juice in the fridge and took a couple of long gulps then threw the rest down the drain. It had a strange aftertaste.

After climbing the stairs to his bedroom, his leg aching, he remembered that he hadn't put chairs in front of the doors. He thought about going back down but figured the deputy would be talking to Ava about now. She wasn't so crazy that she'd come out here tonight. She would know everyone was on to her.

Still, Jace checked to make sure the pistol was under his pillow. His recent wound was bothering him more than he wanted to admit tonight.

As he sat down on the edge of the bed, he

knew it was the confusion in his mind and heart that was really bothering him. Tonight with Kayley and friends had left him aching for something he'd told himself for years he didn't want. Whitehorse. This life. Kayley.

He wanted her more than he had even twelve years ago when he'd been ready to marry her. No one had ever made him feel the way she did.

As he reached to take off his boots, he suddenly felt strange. The room began to spin. He'd had hardly anything to drink tonight, yet he felt drunk. As the room tilted precariously, he had to hold on to the bed to keep from going with it.

His mind raced. What was wrong with him? He remembered the odd taste of the orange juice and fumbled for his cell. The phone slipped from his fingers and fell to the floor. He groped for it.

The room blurred, then dimmed. He fought to stay conscious, but not even his force of will could hold off whatever had been put in the orange juice.

Chapter Eight

Jace bolted upright in bed, his mind a knot of tangled dreams, his head aching and his dry mouth filled with a horrible taste.

As his gaze took in the room, he wondered if it had all been nothing more than a bad dream. Then he smelled her perfume and winced when he realized it was on the bed cover. She'd been in his bed?

He looked down, relieved to see he was still fully clothed.

His mind raced. The last thing he could recall he was starting to take his boots off when he suddenly felt ill and had reached for his phone.

He looked over and saw that his cell phone was sitting on the nightstand. His boots stood side by side over by the chair. No way had he put them there.

His earlier terror came back in a rush as he remembered the strange aftertaste of the orange juice. The woman had drugged him.

Throwing back the covers, he staggered to the bathroom and threw up. Then, after turning on the shower, he stripped down and stood under the beating hot spray until he realized she could still be in the house.

Grabbing a towel, he rushed back into the bedroom to reach for the gun he'd put under his pillow. It was gone.

Nor was he surprised when he quickly dressed and went downstairs to find all signs of the orange juice bottle gone, as well.

He had no proof that he'd been drugged last night. Or that Ava Carris had done it. The only proof he had that someone had been in his room other than the scent of her perfume was his missing gun.

Ava Carris was now armed. He had a feeling she'd always been dangerous.

AVA WOKE CONFUSED. As hard as she tried, she had no memory of last night. She attempted to sit up. Her head swam. Beside the bed, she spotted the empty bottle of wine. Only one glass sat next to it. Had she drunk all of that herself?

She heard a sound in the bathroom and swung her legs over the side of the bed. The dread she felt when she'd awakened grew with each step she took.

At the bathroom door, she turned the knob and pushed. She knew the moment she saw her sister neck deep in bubbles in her motel tub that Evie had done something bad.

"I thought you left," she said, her voice breaking.

"Did you?" Evie blew a handful of bubbles at her and grinned.

Her heart fell. She knew that look. "Oh, Evie, what have you done?"

"Don't you get tired of blaming me for everything?"

"Please tell me you didn't hurt Jace. Oh, please."

"He's more handsome than John," her sister said, making Ava so weak she had to drop the toilet seat and sit. "Too bad he betrayed you and went to the sheriff. The deputy showed me the note you left beside his bed. Really, Ava."

"I didn't want him hurt," she said, barely in a whisper.

"Ava, men always betray you, don't they? Remember what John did?"

She was crying now. "It's not the men. Whenever I like someone, you come along and spoil it." She tore a piece of toilet paper off the roll and blew her nose. "You always have to try to take them away from me." Her voice broke in a sob.

Evie waved a hand through the air, sending bubbles airborne. "Stop blubbering. If you want me to leave…"

Ava couldn't look at her sister. "I want you to leave. I want you out of my head, out of my thoughts." But what difference did it make now? She'd already spoiled everything with Jace. "Just tell me you didn't hurt him."

Evie laughed, and Ava knew she couldn't stand another minute around her. She left the bathroom, suddenly exhausted, and lay down on the bed to rest. When she woke up, her sister was gone, but there was a gun laying on the pillow next to her.

THE FIRST THING SHERIFF McCall Winchester had done this morning after hearing about Jace's call last night in regard to Ava Carris and reading her deputy's report was to get on the phone to Alaska.

She was told by the Anchorage, Alaska, police department that the homicide detective on the case had retired, but most of the information had made the local newspaper—including the original 911 call made by Ava Carris.

Directed to the online site, McCall had become more concerned the more she read. The entire transcript of Ava's hysterical 911 call had indeed made the newspaper.

Caller: "Help me. It's my husband. She killed him."

Dispatcher: "Who killed him?"

Caller: "My sister."

Dispatcher: "Ma'am, is the killer still there?"

Caller: "There's blood all over." Weeping.

Dispatcher: "Ma'am, can you tell me what happened?"

Caller: "I don't know. It's so horrible."

Dispatcher: "Is there anyone else in the house with you?"

Caller: "No, no, Eva left." Hysterical weeping.

Dispatcher: "Ma'am, are there any weapons in the house?"

Caller: "She killed him with a butcher knife." Louder hysterical weeping.

Dispatcher: "The police are on their way. Please don't touch anything. They should be there in just a few minutes. You're sure whoever killed your husband isn't still in the house?"

No answer as the phone was dropped, but what could have been two voices in the background, both female, conversation unintelligible.

"Ma'am? *Ma'am?*" Sirens, then the police pounding on the door and finally breaking it down to find Ava lying next to her husband in a pool of blood, stroking his face with her bloody hand. No sign of another person found in the house.

Shaken by what she'd read, McCall called the former homicide detective at his home.

To her relief, he answered on the third ring. "I just walked in the door. I'm sure when you called my old department they told you that I'm retired. I was out feeding my sled dogs. What can I do for you, Sheriff?"

McCall told him why she was calling. "What

can you tell me about the Ava Carris case? I read some of the news in the papers, but I wanted to talk to you."

"Yeah, it was all in the newspapers, all right," he said. "One of those cases that gets all the media attention because of its bizarre aspects."

"According to what I read, she was raised by a very strict father in the wilderness outside of the city," McCall said. "I didn't see anything about a mother."

"Died, according to the father, in childbirth at the cabin. You should have seen that place. It was nothing but a hole in the wall. Ava had lived there until social services got wind of it and forced him to put her in school."

"How old was she then?"

"Sixteen. She could read and write, but the only book her father had on the premises was the Bible. Why are you asking about Ava?"

"She got out of the mental institution last week and turned up in Whitehorse, Montana."

"I see."

What McCall heard in those two small words only managed to increase her growing anxiety. "She's been stalking one of our residents."

The detective sighed. "That doesn't surprise me. Imagine not seeing anyone other than your father for sixteen years, living in a tiny cabin, being given a daily dose of preaching about sin and damnation. Ava was a shy little thing suddenly thrown into the real world at sixteen. She fell in love almost at once and was married by seventeen. Her father, of course, blamed social services and, as far as I know, never saw her again."

"He disowned her?"

"Well, he never showed up when she was arrested or when she was sent to the state mental hospital."

"I read that she blamed her sister for the murder," McCall said.

He sighed. "Ava swore on the stand that she had a twin sister, but when social services visited the cabin to force her to go to school, the father showed them two graves. One was Ava's mother, who died in childbirth. The other was Ava's twin, who, he told them, had died at the same time as the mother."

McCall could see why this case had gotten so much media attention.

"According to the father, Ava always blamed anything she did wrong on her twin. Classic psychosis according to the mental evaluation that was done on her after her arrest. Some mumbo jumbo about her feeling guilty, blaming herself for her sister's death. For all we know, the father blamed Ava for both her sister's and her mother's deaths."

"What about the husband, John Carris?" McCall asked.

"He apparently was a lot like Ava's father. They lived out in the woods, kept to themselves. They were only married a few months when he was murdered. Stabbed eleven times with a butcher knife. Once, when she was asked why her husband was dead, Ava said because he'd lusted in his heart for her sister but that it hadn't been his fault. She swore her sister always spoiled everything for her."

"Ava was released from the mental hospital after ten years. Now she is stalking a man here in town because he looks like her late husband. Would you consider her dangerous?"

"Wouldn't *you?*"

AVA SQUEEZED HER EYES shut, praying that when she opened her eyes again—

The gun was still lying on the pillow next to her.

She had to get rid of it. It didn't matter where it had come from or what she might have done. She had to—

Goose bumps suddenly prickled her flesh. She squeezed her eyes shut again, pleading to all that was holy for this not to be happening.

She didn't know how much time had passed when she woke in a strange place and heard the creak of the bed frame, felt the bed give as someone sat down on the edge next to her. She groaned inwardly as she smelled the perfume. Her perfume. Evie was wearing the same scent. It filled her nostrils, and she thought she might be sick as her twin whispered, "Hello, Ava" in her ear. "Miss me?"

Keeping her eyes closed, she shook her head hard, afraid to speak.

"I tried to stay away. I really did. Ran out of motels to stay in? I see you rented a house. You weren't hiding from me, were you?" Evie laughed. "Did you really think you could get away from me? I'm always with you. Just like we were in the womb. Together always."

"What do you want?" Ava asked in her little-girl voice as she opened her eyes.

"You know."

"No." She shook her head from side to side.

"I have to take care of the mess you've made," Evie said in disgust. "It's the only way, Ava. Remember how John hurt you? Remember what he did?"

Ava covered her ears with her hands, and yet she could still hear her sister's whisper as if it was in her head.

"This Jace Dennison, he's no different than John. He is lusting after that woman, Kayley Mitchell, just like John lusted after me."

"No, no, no," she cried, but her voice was so weak it couldn't possibly drown out Evie's.

"Don't you want this to end? Imagine how much better you will feel when it's over," her sister said. "You can really start that new life in Seattle. No one need know. I will help you. Haven't I always helped you when you needed me?"

Ava told herself she wasn't listening, but as each word echoed through her, she knew that Evie would have her way. Evie always got what she wanted and had since they were children.

It was Ava who took the blame, got the

strap, made Daddy angry. It was Ava who was forced to stand up all night. It was Ava who got blamed for John's death. Just as she would get blamed for whatever Evie was planning to do now.

JACE TOOK THE KEY OFF the peg by the kitchen side door and drove over to his uncle's house down the road. He'd known where his uncle Audie kept the keys to his gun cabinet since he was ten.

Opening the cabinet, he took out one of his uncle's guns. Audie had a .357 Magnum that would stop a horse. Or a crazy woman, Jace thought as he took the gun and a box of cartridges. He noticed there was one pistol missing. The one his uncle had killed himself with? He felt sick as he closed the cabinet.

Before leaving his house minutes earlier, he'd found how Ava had gotten in last night— through a window at the back of the house. The pane was broken where she had reached in and opened the latch, then climbed in.

As he relocked the gun cabinet, his cell phone rang.

"I saw my deputy's report from last night

about you running into Ava Carris," McCall said when he answered.

Jace heard something in her voice that instantly put him on alert. "I was just coming to see you. She paid me another visit last night. I can't prove it, but she drugged me and took my gun. She gained entry through a window at the back of the house. I just found the broken pane this morning."

"I called the homicide detective who led the John Carris murder case in Alaska," McCall said. "Jace, I'm afraid we have a real psychopath on our hands."

She filled him in, telling him about the way Ava was raised, her mother's and twin's deaths at her birth, the way she had always blamed her sister.

"What was the twin sister's name?" he asked when she finished.

"Eva."

"I met her last night at the bar."

"I beg your pardon?"

"She was completely different from her sister, Ava. I told her I was going to the sheriff if she didn't quit following me, and she broke down and was again the woman I met at the Denver airport."

"They were that different?"

"Spookily so," he said.

"Jace, when Ava called 911 after killing her husband, she said her sister had done it."

"She really does need to be locked up, doesn't she?"

"Not according to the state of Alaska. Jace—"

"I know. Now she's armed and even more dangerous."

"I've put an APB out on her. We'll pick her up and see if we can't get her committed again," the sheriff said. "If not that, then at least hold her on stalking, breaking and entering, and theft."

After he hung up, Jace returned to his house but he was too antsy to sit around. He found himself questioning every decision he'd ever made—especially coming back here. He had to clear his mind, and the last thing he felt like doing was sitting around waiting for Ava Carris to come back.

He saddled up one of the horses in the corral, noticing that the neighbors had been taking care of all the livestock. He'd forgotten how neighbors helped neighbors here.

The air had a bite to it that felt invigorating,

and it was good to be on horseback again as he rode out across the ranch. He wondered why he hadn't done this sooner.

Because he'd forgotten his roots. He smiled at the thought. While it was the first time he'd been on a horse in years, he'd ridden everything from donkeys to yaks to camels and elephants since he'd left Montana.

But he realized he'd missed being on a horse as he rode across the land he would soon sell. It surprised him that the thought made him sad. He'd loved growing up here. Once he'd sold the place, it would be gone. Just like his mother. The mother who had raised him.

The day was too beautiful to think about Virginia Winchester or how badly he'd treated her. None of this was her fault.

It was one of those amazing fall Montana days, the sky a crystalline blue. A few clouds bobbed along high over the rolling prairie. Ahead, a stand of bare-limbed cottonwoods rose up out of the golden horizon.

He knew even before he reached the creek where he was headed. Following the creek bed, he crossed through a narrow underpass under the highway and onto state land until he was riding adjacent to the Mitchell place. He and Kayley used to meet here back when they were kids.

That's why at first he thought he was just imagining her riding across the prairie toward him. He reined in his horse and leaned against the saddle horn as he watched her and realized she hadn't seen him yet.

Her hair flowed back over her shoulders, her face lit with the last of the day's light. If he hadn't already, he would have fallen in love right then. She was so beautiful and looked so free.

She reined in when she saw him, looking startled and nervous. Her eyes were bright and shiny, her face flushed from the ride. He'd never seen her look happier and hoped that seeing him hadn't ruined her horseback ride.

"I never expected to see you here," she said, seeming to regain her composure. "You remembered how to ride?"

He smiled at the challenge in her words. "Just like riding a bike."

She laughed, the sound musical. It pierced his heart. He couldn't bear the thought of never hearing that sound again.

"I remember you on a bicycle," she said smiling at him.

He could see the two of them, just kids trying to learn to ride an old one-speed they'd found in the barn. They'd taken it out to the lane, the ground sun-baked in ruts.

Kayley had run along beside him, keeping him steady until he'd told her to let go, he could do it himself. He smiled now at the memory of hitting a rut and going over the handlebars face-first. Kayley had come running to find him bloody and bruised. He had looked up at her, trying to be tough, not wanting her to see how much it hurt.

She'd stood, hands on her hips, a look in her eye that said: "Why do you have to be so blamed stubborn? You should have let me help you."

"I never did listen to you like I should have," he said now.

"So true," she said with a flip of her hair, her gaze going to the horizon. "Days like this are a gift. I suppose you heard a storm is coming in."

Her gaze came back to him. He nodded. She would have realized that he wanted to be gone by then. He'd never like winters. But after years of spending time in jungles and deserts, the thought of winter seemed almost pleasant.

He instantly imagined sitting in front of a roaring fire with his feet up and Kayley next to him.

"I heard you sold the place," Kayley said, vaporizing the image of the two of them before the fire.

"It's not definite yet."

She raised a brow. "Waiting for a better offer?"

He took off his Stetson and raked a hand through his hair. "Maybe," he said as he settled his hat back on his head.

She smiled, but there was a sadness to it. "Race you to the ridge." She spurred her horse and took off at a gallop.

He charged after her, galloping through the dried golden grass, dust billowing up under his horse's hooves. He heard her laughing as he raced to catch up to her. She sounded out of breath when he finally caught her as they scrambled up a small hill and reined in their horses.

The view from the ridge had always been one of his favorites. He stared out now, Kayley on her horse beside him, and felt his heart kick up a beat at her closeness.

He could see his ranch and hers, the land running wild to the horizon.

His heart began to beat a little faster. How could he leave this place that meant so much to him? Leave this woman again?

"Kayley—"

"I think we should quit meeting like this." Her voice broke. "Don't say something you'll regret later. Please."

He slid off his horse and pulled her to the ground and into his arms. "Kayley." He smothered her protests with a kiss. She fought it for a moment, then softened in his arms, kissing him back as if she thought this might be the last time she ever kissed him.

And then she was pulling away, swinging back up onto her horse and riding away in a cloud of dust. He stood watching her go, the breeze smelling of fall and the coming storm. He feared that would be the last time he would kiss her, maybe even the last time he saw her.

When he checked his cell phone, he found a message from his boss. He was needed back as soon as possible—if he was physically able to do the job. He rubbed his aching leg, but it was his aching heart that was the problem.

When his cell rang, he thought it would be about work.

"You missed your appointment yesterday."

At first Jace didn't recognize the woman's voice.

"To sign the papers for your property?"

He swore. He'd completely forgotten that he was supposed to be in town at two to sign papers. "Something came up. I should have called."

"You forgot." The Realtor sounded disbelieving. "You're the one who wanted to push this through right away. The buyer has been very accommodating."

Yeah, the buyer. Ty Reynolds.

She sighed. "What would be a good time to reschedule? How about this afternoon. Say, four?"

"Sure."

"Mr. Dennison, if you're hoping for another offer—"

"No. I'll be there." He hung up.

TY HADN'T GIVEN ANY MORE thought to the woman he'd seen watching Kayley's house.

He'd been too focused on getting Jace Dennison out of town. He'd nearly lost his mind when Jace hadn't shown up to sign the papers yesterday. Now the Realtor was calling to reschedule?

What the hell was going on? According to the Realtor, Jace had been anxious to sell.

"Does he want more money? Is that it?" he demanded.

"I don't think that's it," the Realtor said. "Apparently he just forgot the appointment."

Like hell.

"He rescheduled for this afternoon. If you could stop by about four."

"Fine. I want this settled."

"I'm sure we can get it all taken care of then," the Realtor assured him.

Except that after he hung up, Ty wasn't assured at all. Was Jace changing his mind?

Kayley. Of course it was about her. Jace was stringing her along. Once he sold the land, she would know he wasn't staying around. But as long as it was in limbo…

He was driving back from checking cattle on his ranch when he drove through the small town of Saco and spotted a silver SUV parked in front of O'Brien's Café. The license plate was out of Billings, and there was a rental sticker on the window.

Even as he turned in and parked, Ty told himself that this was a bad idea. What would be the point of getting into a fight with Jace Dennison? It wouldn't make any points with Kayley, that was for sure.

But at that moment, he didn't give a damn. He was too angry to even care if confronting Jace cost him the property. He just wanted the satisfaction of telling him what a bastard he thought he was.

But as he pushed open the door to the café, he saw at a glance that Jace Dennison wasn't there. Stepping next door to the attached bar, he looked around, wondering how many silver rental SUVs there were.

At least two, he realized as he spotted a familiar face at the far end of the bar.

"Nice to see you again," Ty said as he slid onto the bar stool next to the woman he'd seen watching Kayley's house.

She raised a brow but said nothing as she picked up her drink and took a sip.

"A woman after my own heart," he said and told the bartender he'd take what the lady was having.

"Who said I was a lady?"

He chuckled as he took a good look at the woman. With chin-length dark hair cut in a bob and wide, golden brown eyes, she was strikingly attractive. Her jeans and T-shirt hugged some very interesting curves.

"I get the feeling we have a lot in common," Ty said after the bartender slid a margarita in front of him. "What shall we drink to?"

"What makes you think I want to drink with you?" she asked coyly.

"Apparently, other than margaritas, we have Kayley Mitchell in common. I saw you spying on her the other night."

"Really?"

"Yeah. So, what do we drink to?" he asked again, holding up his glass.

"Getting to know each other better," she said and gently touched her glass to his. "I didn't catch your name."

"Ty. Ty Reynolds."

She smiled. "Nice to meet you, Ty. You can call me Eva."

Chapter Nine

Kayley was furious with herself. Back at the house, she sat down and finished off the cake from the previous night. It didn't make her feel any better.

She wasn't angry at herself for kissing Jace. She actually smiled as she scraped the cake pan and took the last bite before carrying the pan over to the sink. She loved kissing Jace, loved making love with him, simply loved him.

But Ty was right about one thing: she felt herself getting drawn back in. From the moment she knew he would be coming home and that she would probably see him, Kayley had been clear on one point: she wasn't going to let Jace break her heart again.

She really had believed she was prepared to not let that happen. But she'd let him get closer than she'd planned. Now the thought of never seeing him again made her ache inside.

She touched her lips with her fingertips, remembering the kiss, remembering the look in his eyes, and snatched up the phone.

"I think Jace is having doubts about leaving, and it is making me crazy," she said the moment her friend Shawna answered.

"Didn't I warn you that this was going to happen? You have to stay away from him."

"How do you suggest I do that in a town the size of Whitehorse? I was out riding my horse—"

"Where you and Jace used to ride together? Kayley!"

"I didn't know he would be there. I'm telling you the truth. I got the feeling he'd left his cowboy days behind him."

"Apparently not. When is he leaving?"

"I don't know."

"Don't you have a four-day weekend starting tomorrow?"

Teachers got two personal days this week, which meant the students did, too.

"Tell Jace that you're going away," Shawna said. "Far enough that there is no chance he is going to find you."

"I can't leave right now. I have way too much to do here to get ready for the holidays and school and—"

"But Jace doesn't know that. Hide your pickup in the garage. Don't answer your phone. It will be a good test for both of you."

Shawna had a point. It would also keep Ty away. She would tell everyone she was going to Billings to stay with a friend down there and shop.

"You will both have time to think about what is really going on," her friend said.

Kayley nodded to herself, even though she knew that when she surfaced again Jace could be gone. But it was for the best. "I'll do it."

The first call she placed was to one of the biggest gossips in town. Then she called Andi. She thought about calling Jace, but decided it would be best if he heard it through someone else and asked Andi to have Cade tell Jace, if he wouldn't mind.

When she called Ty, he didn't pick up. She didn't leave a message.

JACE WAS SURPRISED WHEN he reined in at his corral to find Cade waiting for him.

"I brought over some tamales Andi made,"

his friend said as he watched Jace unsaddle his horse. "I thought we could have an early supper."

They sat down in the shade of the back patio and ate the still-warm tamales with a couple of cold beers that Cade had also bought.

"Why don't you tell me why you really stopped by?" Jace asked after they'd eaten.

"I'm sorry about the other night after dinner at the house," Cade said. "I was out of the line. The women gave me hell."

Jace laughed. "You were right." He took a breath and let it go as he looked out across the pasture. "I'm still in love with Kayley."

His friend laughed. "Like that is a surprise to anyone."

"I don't want her waiting for me again."

"Have you told her that?" Cade asked.

Now it was Jace's turn to laugh. "Hell, she's the one who told me. Not in so many words, but she's determined not to hear how I feel about her."

Cade shook his head and finished his beer.

"I went for a horseback ride earlier," Jace said into the silence. "I thought I no longer had any connection to this place, this land. It made me sad to think about selling it."

"You know, if I had this land, I'd tear down both houses. I think it would save money in the long run since neither is energy efficient. That rise over there would be a great place to build a house," Cade said. "Nice view of the river. Bet that field would be full of whitetail deer in the mornings during hunting season."

"Are you thinking about making an offer?" Jace asked, pretending he didn't know what his friend was saying.

"What will you do with the money from the sale?" Cade asked.

"If you're asking if I need the money, I don't. I haven't taken up gambling or drugs or expensive hobbies."

"No, I would imagine you travel light," Cade agreed. "Maybe you should stay away from her until you figure a few things out."

"Yeah." He thought about seeing her riding toward him, about the kiss on the high ridge, about watching her ride away. He knew whatever decision he made this time, there would be no going back.

His friend sighed. "I brought over supper because I had a message for you from Kayley via Andi. She's taking off for a few days. She told Andi, who told me to tell you."

Jace chuckled. "So that's what the tamales were about. I should always get my news via tamales, then. They were delicious. Thank Andi for me."

He didn't need Andi or Cade to tell him why Kayley was leaving. She expected him to be gone before she got back. She didn't want to see him again.

He knew that was probably for the best. So why did he feel as if he'd been kicked in the chest by a horse? "Is Ty going with her?" he managed to ask around the lump that had formed in his throat.

Cade shrugged as he got to his feet. "It's been nice having you back in town."

"Yeah, it was," Jace said, rising to shake his friend's hand.

"It's not too late to change your mind," Cade said.

Jace nodded, but he feared it was. Even if Kayley could forgive him for what he did to her twelve years ago, he wasn't sure he could forgive himself.

VIRGINIA FOUND HER MOTHER in the parlor, staring into the fire that burned on the grate. She often found Pepper Winchester like this.

If she had had to guess what her mother was thinking about, she would have figured Trace. Virginia had come to understand since being here that her mother would never get over her youngest son's murder.

"Mind if I join you?" she asked.

Pepper looked up. It took her a moment to focus on her only daughter. Virginia was the oldest of the five siblings, and she and her mother had never been close.

Had she thought that coming back to the ranch might change that, Virginia would have been sorely disappointed.

Her mother motioned to the chair next to her. "I heard there is a winter storm warning. Has it started to snow yet?"

"No. Not until later. But something is definitely blowing in." This was the kind of conversation they often had. The weather was the only thing they could talk about without arguing.

"I don't mind the snow," Pepper said. "It's that darned wind. It always blows in the road, and without Alfred here to run the plow—"

"I can run the plow."

Her mother looked over at her, clearly amused. "You?"

"You've always underestimated me, Mother. Haven't you wondered how I managed to survive the past twenty-seven years without you and the Winchester money?" She waved a hand through the air as if swatting away that particular topic.

"That is not what I wanted to talk to you about," she said before she and her mother could get into a fight.

"Let me guess—you want to talk about money."

Virginia smiled ruefully. That was always at the heart of it—the Winchester fortune—if there was any left.

"In a way, that *is* what I wanted to talk to you about," she admitted. "But not in the way you think. I want you to acknowledge my son."

Pepper had turned her attention back to the fire but now swiveled around to stare at her daughter.

"I want Jace to have whatever you might have left me," she said.

Pepper seemed speechless.

"I know you think the only reason I came back was because I thought you were dying and wanted my share of whatever is left here,"

Virginia said. "I wasn't fighting for the money. I was fighting for my place in this family, and I equated that with getting a fair share of the inheritance."

Her mother started to speak, but she stopped her.

"Jace Dennison is my son. I don't want him to feel left out the way I have my whole life. He's a Winchester. I want you to promise me that you will accept him—if not now, then on your deathbed."

"You would give up your share of the Winchester fortune for your son?" Pepper asked, sounding astonished.

Virginia rose to her feet. "Do I have your promise?"

"Yes," her mother said, looking at her as if seeing her for the first time.

WHEN JACE HEADED INTO town to the Realtor's office later that afternoon, he noticed that Kayley's pickup was gone, the blinds closed, no sign of life.

She must have already left on her trip.

All his instincts told him not to do this, as he parked in front of the real estate office and sat asking himself what the hell he was doing.

After a few moments, he got out and went inside.

"I know I'm late but we need to talk," he told his Realtor as she led him into her office and closed the door.

"Yes, we do," she agreed, not sounding happy. "The buyer didn't show this afternoon."

He stared at her. "He backed out?"

She shrugged. "Maybe he's just trying to get back at you for not showing up yesterday and accepting his offer, or maybe he's changed his mind. I personally thought his offer was a little high."

Jace laughed; he couldn't help himself.

"I'm sorry, but I fail to see what is funny about all this."

"I was just sitting outside trying to talk myself into going through with this deal."

"Well, now there is no deal, apparently."

"My point exactly." He stood to leave. "Looks like things have taken care of themselves."

"You would be a fool to take your property off the market right now," she said.

"Believe me, it won't be the first time I've been a fool. Or probably the last."

"I'm sure the buyer will come back with another offer," she said. "Why don't you let me try to get hold of him again? He doesn't seem to be answering his cell phone, but I'm sure—"

"I'm sorry, but I've decided I'm going to hang on to the property for the time being," Jace said. Staying in Whitehorse wouldn't be easy. He'd have to accept that he was a Winchester.

But he wasn't worried about any of that right now. Fighting to get Kayley back was going to be the hard part.

As Ty looked at the woman on the barstool next to him, he wondered what he'd ever seen in Kayley. She'd always been in love with Jace Dennison. Why had he spent years waiting for her to get over him?

It made no sense, especially when a woman like the one sitting next to him was so beautiful and interested in him—if her hand on his thigh was any indication.

"Let's have another drink, then get out of here," she whispered in his ear.

"Sounds good to me." He was all grins. Even the bartender was giving him a look like he was one lucky SOB.

"You never told me why you were watching

Kayley Mitchell's house," he said, realizing he was starting to feel the drinks he'd consumed.

"Maybe it wasn't her I was watching," she said with a come-hither look.

"*Me?*"

"I've always wanted a cowboy."

He laughed, delighted. "Well, honey, that's just what I am." Not a rodeo cowboy like Jace had been. No, Ty had been too busy actually cowboying on his old man's spread. "Want to guess how many cattle I run?"

Their drinks arrived, and he excused himself to go to the men's room. He felt a little unsteady on his feet, but nothing to worry about. If there was one thing he could do, it was hold his liquor.

When he returned, Eva had already consumed half of her drink. He admired the devil out of her. The woman sure could hold her booze. She didn't even look tipsy.

"Drink up, Ty," she whispered as he slid onto his stool. "The night is young. I have something special I want to do with you."

By the time they left the bar, he was feeling no pain—and the winter storm had blown in, already dropping a good six inches while they'd been in the bar. Not only that, it was getting dark. Ty hadn't realized it was so late. He had a nagging feeling that he'd forgotten something.

"You'd better let me drive," she said and took the keys from him.

He was about to protest, when he had to grab the side of his pickup to stay on his feet. "Whoa, you might be right about driving. You ever drive in a snowstorm, though?" Huge flakes pelted them, the wind blowing the snow horizontally across the road. "The visibility is going to be bad."

"Not to worry. There isn't much I can't do," she assured him.

He believed it.

She opened the pickup door, and he managed to climb into the passenger side. He couldn't believe how dizzy he felt, and the blinding snowstorm only made him feel more disoriented.

"You never told me," Eva said as she climbed behind the wheel. "What were you doing hiding in the trees by Kayley Mitchell's that night?"

"She and I used to date," he said, slurring his words. He lay back, having trouble focusing as she started his pickup engine and hit the windshield wipers.

As she pulled out onto the highway, snow whipped past in a white blur. He couldn't even be sure they were going in the right direction.

"You sure you can see the road?" he asked. Or at least he thought he did.

When she didn't answer, he glanced over at her. She seemed intent on her driving. Good. He closed his eyes, telling himself he would just take a little rest.

As she'd said, the night was young, and Kayley Mitchell was just a distant memory. It was the last thought he had before Ava woke him a while later.

Chapter Ten

"Ty Reynolds's pickup was found north of town in a ditch," the dispatcher said. "A neighbor just called it in. The truck cab's empty. No sign of him."

McCall shook her head. It had been like that all morning, one call after another of someone off the road, fender benders, people stuck. This always happened the first big snowstorm of the season.

"No sign of Ty?" she asked.

The dispatcher shook her head as she handed the sheriff the location of Ty's pickup. "Everyone on duty is out on a call."

"I'll take it," she said, surprised to see where he'd gone off the road. "What the devil was he doing out there in a blizzard?" The sheriff sighed and radioed the two deputies who'd been on call all morning because of the storm.

"Ty Reynolds's pickup was found north of town in a ditch," she said. "We need to find out if anyone has seen him or if we need to start looking for him in a snowdrift out that way. I'm going to make a few calls. Let me know if you hear anything. The closest farmhouse is a good five miles up the road."

Ty lived alone on one of his ranches outside of town. There was no answer at his house. She called a couple of places in town where he often had coffee in the morning, but no one had seen him.

She'd just hung up when she got a call from one of her deputies.

"I just talked to my friend who bartends out in Saco," he said. "Ty's kind of a regular out there. He was in yesterday afternoon drinking margaritas. He left just after dark. With a woman."

McCall swore under her breath and hoped they weren't looking for two bodies in a snow-bank. Most everyone knew to stay with their vehicles if they went off the road in a storm like this one. Ty should have been that smart, but if he'd been drinking...

"Did your friend give you a description

of the woman?" She listened with growing concern as he described Ava Carris.

"Isn't this the woman we have an APB out on?"

"It sounds like it. What about her vehicle? Is it still at the bar?" McCall didn't have to describe the silver SUV—that information had already gone out to law enforcement.

The deputy left the line but returned a few moments later. "No sign of the SUV, but she was driving it when she arrived at the bar. She left driving Ty's pickup, though."

A NIGHT TERROR WOKE AVA. She jerked up in bed feeling as if she were climbing out of a dense fog. Why had she been sleeping so much lately? And drinking? She dragged herself out of the bed and staggered to the bathroom to be sick.

As she turned on the shower, thankful not to find Evie either sitting on the edge of her bed or soaking in her bathtub, Ava felt the affects of a night filled with nightmares. She remembered that her father had night terrors. She had been told by her psychiatrist at the institution that they were a neurological condition that ran in families. Genetic.

Her head ached, her mouth dry as a cotton

ball, her stomach queasy again as she stepped into the shower. Had Evie drugged her again?

The thought terrified her. If Evie had needed to get her out of the way, then she must have been doing something awful.

She showered quickly and turned off the faucet. As she drew back the shower curtain, Ava was terrified she would find her sister standing there.

The bathroom was empty. She breathed a sigh of relief. Maybe Evie had gotten tired of tormenting her and really left. Ava knew that she could never get well as long as Evie was hanging around.

As she came out of the bathroom, she felt a little better. It was cold in the small old house she'd rented. She turned up the heat and had a vague memory of it storming last night, snow blowing across the road. She frowned. How did she know that? Had she looked out the window?

That's when she saw her boots. They sat just inside the front door—in a puddle of water.

Her heart skipped to a stop. Had she gone out last night?

No, she wouldn't have gone out in a storm

like the one that had blown in. She'd stood at the window and watched the snow come down.

Then how did her boots get wet?

She backed away from the sight of her wet boots and bumped into the table. Something rustled behind her. She turned slowly, fear making her breath come in gasps.

Ava stared at what sat in the middle of the table. A paper sack. She didn't remember putting it there, and the sight of it filled her with fear that she might have done something regrettable last night. Why had she listened to Evie?

Ava had wanted to leave town and forget about Jace Dennison, but Evie had stopped her.

"You go ahead and leave, but *I'm* staying."

She'd known from the way her sister had said it that she wasn't going to leave Jace alone. "If I stay, will you promise to behave?"

She tried to calm down. Maybe Evie had stopped by and brought her donuts from the local market. Or a quart of orange juice like Jace had bought.

Fingers trembling, she pinched the top edge

of the paper sack and pulled it down to look inside.

A scream caught in her throat. She jerked back, dragging the sack with her. The contents tumbled onto the worn carpet at her feet.

Ava stared at the bloody knife with a horrifying sense of déjà vu.

KAYLEY REGRETTED HER plan almost at once. Hiding out from Jace made her feel like a coward. She'd always been honest about her feelings for him—at least with herself.

When the phone rang, she saw it was Andi and quickly picked up.

"I sent Cade over to tell Jace for you."

"And?"

"And they ate the tamales I sent, and Jace left to go sign papers to sell the property. I'm so sorry, Kayley."

Kayley nodded to herself. "So I shouldn't have bothered to pretend to leave town."

"Jace did ask if Ty was going with you."

She wasn't surprised. "Yeah, his interest in me increased substantially when he thought there was someone else."

"That means he still cares about you. Look, I said I'd help you, but I think this is a mistake.

Go to Jace. Tell him how you feel. Cade says he doesn't think Jace wants to leave. He's really torn. If you talk to him—"

"Andi, I know he's having second thoughts, but he has to work this out on his own. I tried to stop him from leaving twelve years ago. This time it has to be Jace who wants to stay badly enough that he can put the past behind him. Things are worse here for him than they were the last time he left."

"Nothing is worse than losing your father, then your baby," Andi said.

"Maybe not. But learning that Marie wasn't his mother and all of that about his uncle...."

"Jace is strong. Cade said he thinks he's having trouble forgiving himself for leaving you when you were in as much pain as he was."

That sounded like Jace. "This really has to be his decision. He has to want to stay more than...more than taking his next breath." There was a knock at the door. "Listen, I have to go, someone is here." She hung up. Another knock, this one more persistent.

She glanced out and saw a silver SUV parked in front of her house.

Jace!

Her heart raced at the thought. Was it possible he'd come by to tell her he was staying? Not just staying, but that he wanted the two of them to start over?

Isn't this what she'd dreamed? That he would realize the mistake he'd made and come sweep her off her feet?

But as she opened the door, Kayley saw it wasn't Jace.

She frowned, at first not recognizing the slight, dark-haired woman standing before her.

It was only when she saw the gun that Kayley remembered that this had been the woman she'd seen following her and later watching her at the school. By then it was too late.

MCCALL GAVE JACE a call and was relieved when he answered on the first ring.

"You found Ava," he said hopefully.

"No, I'm sorry." She told him what she knew about Ty.

"You don't think…"

"I'm going out to where his pickup was found and look for him," McCall said.

"Kayley hasn't heard from him?" Jace asked.

"I hadn't thought to call her."

"I think she left yesterday before the storm to go to Billings to stay with a friend for a few days, but I might run by there just in case," Jace said.

McCall hung up. She hadn't told Jace to be careful since she knew he would be. Wasn't he trained for this sort of thing?

She drove north, the landscape a mask of brilliant white. The sun had come out, making the new snow sparkle like diamonds. It was blinding and beautiful and deadly if you ended up out in it without the proper clothing.

Last night's storm had been a blizzard with freezing temperatures and a wind-chill factor down to twenty below zero. If Ty was out in it for very long, she was looking for his body.

But was she looking for just him? she wondered as she headed down the narrow road where his pickup had been found in the ditch. Why would Ty drive down this way?

The bartender had told her deputy that Ty wasn't driving. Ava had been driving. She didn't know the area. Maybe she turned down the wrong road.

She found Ty's pickup in the ditch and, leaving her patrol SUV running, got out to look inside it. The driver's-side door was open. She took a look inside, hoping to find something that would give her a clue what might have happened on this road last night.

The first thing that hit her was the distinct smell of perfume. She reared back at the strong scent and noticed that the keys were still in the ignition. Her pulse quickened. Ty wouldn't have left his keys.

Finding nothing else in the pickup to help her, McCall climbed back into her patrol SUV and, bucking snowdrifts, drove slowly up the road.

She hadn't gone far when she saw the birds.

They were feeding on something a dozen yards off the road, the black birds stark against the pristine snow.

She parked and got out to survey the landscape for a moment before she started through the drifted snow.

Several of the birds flapped a few feet away from whatever they'd been pecking, but several turned beady dark eyes on her and refused to be frightened away from whatever they'd found half buried in a drift.

McCall stopped for a moment, again surveying the frozen expanse. Any sign of footprints would have been destroyed by the blowing snow. Even wearing sunglasses, her eyes hurt from the sun reflecting off the snow. The sky was a pale light white. Everything glistened, including the birds as she advanced on them.

One of the birds let out a squawk, and McCall saw what they had been feeding on. The body lay facedown in the snow. Down feathers lifted into the air from holes pecked in the jacket the victim had been wearing.

McCall called for backup, shooing away the birds and finally firing her gun into the air to scatter them.

As she stepped closer, she saw that among the holes the birds had made there were short slices in the jacket fabric.

Her heart began to pound. Stab wounds?

Chapter Eleven

Kayley hurt all over. She licked at her split lip, knowing her problems were much worse than a few cuts and bruises.

She had underestimated this woman, she thought, studying her. She wouldn't make that mistake again.

Not that she would get the chance.

When she'd opened her door, recognized the woman and seen the gun, she'd reacted instinctively by slamming the door and trying to get it closed and locked.

But the woman was stronger than she had looked for her size and had forced her way in before Kayley could get the door closed all the way.

She'd left Kayley no choice but to make a run for it, tearing through the house toward the back door off the kitchen. All the way, she'd expected to hear the sound of gunfire and feel the burn of a bullet.

But the woman hadn't shot her.

She had come after her, though, before Kayley could get to the back door. They had struggled, with Kayley grabbing anything she could to use as a weapon to hold her off, pulling down whatever was on the kitchen counter.

But the woman was tenacious, with a freakish kind of strength that terrified her. She'd fought for her life, seeing something in the woman's eyes that told her just because she hadn't shot her didn't mean she wasn't still planning to kill her.

At one point in their struggle, the woman had backhanded her with the pistol. Kayley had blacked out, only to surface to find her hands duct-taped behind her and the woman standing over her with the teapot and pouring cold water into her face.

"Jace didn't tell me you were such a fighter," the woman said.

Kayley licked her lip and tasted blood. Her headed ached and her nose was bleeding. "You know Jace?" She realized she shouldn't have been surprised. The woman had shown up about the same time as Jace, and she was driving a vehicle like his. Kayley had thought several times that it was Jace's rental SUV only to realize it was the woman—a woman who'd followed her one day and spied on her the next.

Kayley had felt so safe in Whitehorse that she hadn't thought that much of it. Until now.

"Of course I know Jace," the woman said, smiling. "He's my husband."

Kayley thought she must have heard wrong. "That can't be true."

"Just because he didn't tell you about me?" The woman laughed. "Maybe he's been trying to find a way to tell you since he came home."

That struck her like another blow. Did this explain the battle she'd felt going on in Jace?

"It's been very difficult for him. He knows how close you and his mother were, and with his mother dying—"

"He told you Marie and I were close?"

"He told me *everything*," the woman said. "Jace is dealing with a lot of guilt. He didn't just leave you when he left Whitehorse. He feels bad about not getting home before his mother died. Then there is the guilt he feels over you."

All these things were true; Kayley knew because she *knew* Jace, knew him in a way that had always been a special bond between them. She stared at the woman, her heart breaking. "Who—"

"I'm sorry, I should have introduced myself. I'm Ava Dennison. I hate to have to be the one to tell you all this. Jace… Well, you know how he is. His mother knew he was running away when he left. I'm sure she mentioned that to you. She did to Jace. He's told me how he ran away from the pain twelve years ago."

Kayley wasn't sure what shocked her more. That this woman knew all these intimate things about Jace and her and the family. Or that the woman Jace had married had beaten her, bound her and was now holding a gun to her head.

Her head ached, but her mind rebelled at even the thought that Jace could have married this woman. And yet how did she explain this otherwise?

"I can imagine how heartbroken you were when Jace left you, especially since you'd just lost your baby," Ava was saying.

Kayley felt tears well and spill from her eyes. Jace had told her about the baby? Only a few people knew about her miscarriage. Or how heartbroken they had both been.

"You can understand why he couldn't find the words to tell you about him and me," the woman was saying. "But now that I'm having his baby...."

No. Kayley shut her eyes tight, fighting the tears. This wasn't happening. "What do you want with me?" she asked, feeling all of the fight go out of her.

"You have to let him go."

She opened her eyes and looked up at the woman standing over her. "I have."

"No," the woman said with a rueful smile as she knelt down in front of Kayley. "Sleeping with him isn't letting him go. As long as you are always there for him, he only feels more guilty about what he did to you. You can't be there for him anymore."

"I won't."

"I know." Ava smiled. "Now get up. We're going to take a ride."

"No," Kayley said, realizing she had no choice. But she feared she'd never come back if she went anywhere with this woman.

"Don't be silly. We're just going to meet Jace. He won't be happy that we fought and that you got hurt, but he knows he has to end this with you. He has to tell you about us, about our baby, about our life far away from here and how you can't be a part of it."

"I don't believe we're going to meet Jace."

The woman reached for something on the kitchen counter, then surprised Kayley by grabbing a handful of her hair. She jerked Kayley's head back, making her cry out in pain.

"I don't want to hurt you, but I will if you force me to. Now, let me help you up."

Kayley felt the painful, sharp tip of a knife pressed against her throat.

"Gently," Ava said. "Knives are so dangerous if you don't know how to use them. Fortunately for you, I am very good with knives."

McCALL WAS WAITING outside the autopsy room when coroner George Murphy came out. "Well?"

George shook his head in obvious amusement. He was a large, young, florid-faced man who'd thrown up at his first murder scene—not that she'd ever told anyone. McCall had expected him to have quit by now, as squeamish as he was.

"There is something macabre about always finding you waiting here." She'd never been able to wait for the official report to get typed up, and since the local coroner assisted with the autopsies, she could get a jump on things by grilling him right away.

"Well?" she repeated, anxious to get moving again. Ava Carris was still missing. The crime techs had scoured the area where Ty Reynolds's body had been found. No Ava.

Which was no surprise to McCall. She just worried where Ava would turn up next. She'd called Jace and warned him. Last she'd heard from him, he'd gone to check on Kayley, although he was sure she'd driven to Billings yesterday to spend a few days with a friend.

McCall had been glad to hear that, though she worried that Jace was in more trouble than he realized. Apparently Ava's diminutive size and apparently sweet-looking face had fooled Ty. She hoped Jace was smarter.

"Cause of death," she said impatiently now to the coroner.

"Overdose of a strong barbiturate. The lab

will have to run the toxicology before we know what, exactly. "

McCall blinked in surprise. "I saw knife wounds."

"Uh-huh. But they didn't kill him. The large quantity of drugs he'd ingested killed him before the stab wounds, while deadly, could do him in."

McCall rocked back, trying to make sense of this. "Why stab him if he was almost dead?"

"To make a point?"

"George, was that a pun? You're starting to like this job," she joked.

"Not likely. Why is it that the moment I become coroner, people start getting murdered?" He shook his big head. "The coroner from the crime lab is finishing up. I'm sure his report will be on your desk by this afternoon. I'm going back to bed."

McCall watched him shuffle down the hall. Ava Carris couldn't have carried Ty out into the field where McCall had found his body. That meant he'd gone out there with her. She shook her head, trying to imagine a scenario where a man would follow a woman out into a snowstorm.

Apparently Ava Carris was very persuasive.

It didn't skip her mind that Ava had murdered her husband with a butcher knife. Eleven stab wounds.

"George," she called after him. "How many stab wounds?"

He turned to look at her as if her question was too ghoulish for the hour of the morning. "Eleven." He yawned, turned and left.

JACE KNEW THAT KAYLEY wouldn't be home. Cade had told him she'd left town for a few days. He'd thought she'd probably left with Ty. That would explain why Ty hadn't shown up at the Realtor's office.

But now, knowing that Ty hadn't been with Kayley but instead had been with Ava—

He'd had to bust through snowdrifts to get out of his road to the highway and had expected to have to do the same when he reached Kayley's. But as he slowed to turn onto her road, he saw that a vehicle had already been down the road. Twice, it appeared.

Or someone had been in and out this morning.

He'd been so sure Kayley had left yesterday,

he hadn't called her. He'd decided that these four days she was gone, he would get some things taken care of, get his head on straight.

Putting off the sale of his property had been the first step.

Now, as he drove into Kayley's yard and parked, he could see that the blinds were closed, no lights on inside.

Still, he climbed out, noticing the footprints in the snow. Small tracks. Like a woman's. Was it possible Kayley had asked one of her friends to come over and watch the place while she was gone?

He glanced first toward the garage and made his way over there to find Kayley's pickup sitting in the dim darkness inside.

What the hell?

Maybe she went to Billings with a friend, he told himself as he walked up the porch steps. At the door, he knocked. Of course, no one answered. Then he peered in the window through a crack in the blind, feeling like a Peeping Tom but unable to shake the bad feeling he'd gotten the moment he'd seen that someone had been down the road this morning.

The living room looked just as it had the night he'd visited Kayley, nothing out of place, everything neat and clean. No wonder his mother had loved this woman and wanted him to marry her, he thought, trying to shake off his growing uneasiness.

He moved down the porch to peek in the kitchen window. With a start, he saw that one of the stools was lying on its side, a pan next to it.

His heart began to pound. Kayley would never leave her kitchen like that. He hurried back to the door. The knob turned in his hand. She hadn't locked the door—even though she had left town for a few days?

Alarm bells went off in his head as he moved quickly to the kitchen, only to find broken dishes on the floor and a trail of smeared blood.

"Kayley!" he called as he ran through the house, praying she was here, all the time knowing she wasn't. "Kayley!" She wasn't in the house.

He told himself maybe she'd cut herself, called a friend and was on her way to the hospital at this very moment.

Jace reached for his cell phone.

But before he could make the call, his phone

rang. *Let it be Kayley. Let there be a good explanation for what I'm seeing.*

But as he answered, he felt his stomach drop at the sound of Ava Carris's voice on the other end of the line. He'd known even before she told him.

Ava had Kayley.

Chapter Twelve

Jace felt his guts liquefy at Ava's words.

"I have Kayley. If you don't want her death on your conscience, then you will do exactly as I say."

His throat ached from the fear. "Don't hurt her."

"That's up to you. If you betray me again by going to the sheriff, I won't have any choice." She sounded as if she was talking about taking in a movie. Her lack of emotion terrified him all the more.

"I won't do that. I promise. Just tell me where to meet you. I'll come alone."

"Good. We're waiting for you. I've had a lot of time on my hands, so I've been reading up on the history of your hometown and the area around it."

She sounded so damned normal that he had

to shake himself. What the hell was she talking about?

"I'm fascinated by the gold rush and these old gold mines around here," Ava was saying. "Do you know the one north of your ranch?"

His heart was pounding. "That mine is dangerous."

"But you like danger. Isn't that why you left Whitehorse to become a spy?"

"I'm not a spy."

"No, you're like some undercover James Bond."

"Hardly."

"Oh, don't be modest. You're a hero. But I must warn you not to try anything heroic with me. I don't want to kill Kayley, but you know I will if you force me to. Do we understand each other?"

She was playing with him. "Yes, we understand each other perfectly." He would strangle this woman with his bare hands when he got hold of her.

"I'm looking forward to seeing you again," she said. "We have had so little time to just talk. I really think you will find that we have a lot in common."

He swore silently. "I'm headed toward the

mine right now. I just want to make sure we're talking about the same one."

"It's the one you and Kayley used to ride your horses to when you were kids."

He caught his breath. How…? Of course. She'd been in his house numerous times. She'd had a key made. She'd put away his clothing, left him presents. Why hadn't he realized she wouldn't hesitate to go through his mother's things, especially her photo albums of him and Kayley? And all those letters she saved not only from him but from Kayley.

He cursed himself for not realizing that Ava Carris's obsession with him might lead her to Kayley.

"I was so sorry to hear about the baby you and Kayley lost."

Jace felt an icy steel shaft of fury move through him. He warned himself not to let his emotions make him more careless and stupid than he had been already. He had to think like the operative he was. The problem was that those jobs hadn't been personal. This was beyond personal. A crazy woman had Kayley.

"I want to speak to Kayley."

"Now, Jace, you don't get to ask for anything."

"I speak to Kayley, or I'm not meeting you at the mine." He had to demand proof of life, and yet he realized he wasn't dealing with a normal kidnapper. He wasn't dealing with normal at all.

He listened to the silence, his heart in this throat, petrified that she'd hung up on him. That she would just kill Kayley out of spite. That he'd blown it.

"I'll have to get her. You don't mind holding, do you?"

"I'll be right here." He drove down the road and turned in at the mailbox that read Dennison, his mind racing as to what to take up to the mine. He would have to be ready for anything. A mind like Ava's could be diabolical in its complexity for deception, for intrigue, for cruelty.

All his instincts told him she would want to punish him. She knew about him and Kayley, knew that they'd gotten close again.

He couldn't keep beating himself up over that. He'd let a woman like Ava Carris get so close that she now was holding the only woman he'd ever loved hostage.

Whatever it took, he would free Kayley—or die trying.

He'd just entered his uncle's house when he heard Ava come back on the phone.

"Keep it short," he heard her say.

"Jace."

He closed his eyes at the sound of Kayley's voice, trying to breathe with his heart near bursting. If Ava didn't kill her, Kayley could be killed in a cave-in. That mine tunnel was as unstable as Ava Carris.

"It's okay," he said, fighting to keep his voice from giving away his emotions. "I'm coming for you."

"No Jace, she's—"

He winced at the sound of Kayley's cry, fisting his free hand in fury.

"I'm getting impatient, Jace," Ava said in her soft, innocent voice after just hurting Kayley. "I don't think you want me to have too much time on my hands, now, do you?"

"No." It was all he could do not to reach through the phone for the bitch's throat. "I should be there within twenty minutes. I'll call back in ten minutes to make sure Kayley is still able to speak on the phone."

Ava chuckled. "Okay, Jace, but that won't be

necessary. We'll all be here waiting for you. Did I mention that my sister is here? She has the worst crush on you, so this should be very interesting. All these women willing to die for you."

He heard Ava make a sound like she'd just had the air knocked out of her. He could hear a struggle in the background. "Ava? *Ava?*" The phone went dead.

Even more worried now, Jace moved quickly through the house. His uncle Audie had been a hunter and active outdoorsman. Everything Jace might need inside the tunnel was here.

Rope. Small, folding shovel. Headlamp. Weapons.

He'd never told his mother, but Uncle Audie had once taken him inside the mine. That alone should have panicked Jace, since he knew how dangerous it was. He and Audie had set off a cave-in by accident and had to dig their way out.

They'd been lucky. Jace hoped to hell that luck held today.

He filled an old backpack, taking the .357 Magnum but knowing that would be the first thing Ava would insist on taking from him. He holstered it and grabbed one of his uncle's hunting knives, then a smaller, sleeker one for inside his boot, thinking about how much Ava apparently enjoyed knives.

Ava would expect him to be armed.

He didn't want to disappoint her.

Slinging the backpack strap over his shoulder, Jace headed for his uncle's three-quarter-ton, four-wheel-drive pickup. He wanted to make sure he didn't get stuck going out to the mine. He couldn't take any chances with Kayley's safely.

He tried not think about what Ava had done to her so far. Or what he was going to do to Ava. One thing was certain. Ava Carris would never have to worry about being sent back to a mental institution.

As he drove toward the foothills where the gold mines had been dug deep into the cold darkness of the hillside, he tried to reassure himself that Kayley was all right. She was the strongest woman he'd ever known. That scene back at her kitchen proved that she wouldn't go down without a fight.

He felt the lump rise in his throat as he recalled how she had tried to warn him not to come for her. He shook his head, amazed at the irony of it.

It had taken him so long to admit to the mistake he'd made twelve years ago. Kayley had waited for him because she'd known they belonged together. She'd never lost faith in them. In him.

After all these years of fighting it, he now knew that he wanted her more than life itself—and he was going to have to prove it. Because if he wasn't the best trained killer he could be, Kayley was going to die.

"WE FOUND THE HOUSE Ava has been renting," the deputy said when the sheriff answered.

It had been the craziest of mornings after the big storm. Normally there were the usual accidents, people snowed in and needing help. This morning McCall had a murder on her hands—and a missing psychopath. On top of that she had two different parties stranded to the south by Fourchette Bay down on Fort Peck Reservoir.

Both had campers, food and fuel and said they could last for several days, so she'd kept her deputies working on the murder case—and searching for Ava Carris.

The county would be plowing, getting roads open, and all other law enforcement—including her game-warden fiancé, Luke Crawford—were helping in the search for Ava or assisting motorists.

"It's over here in Dobson," the deputy said.

"I'll be right there."

McCall made the drive in thirty minutes even on the snow-packed, slick road. She felt as if a clock was ticking, no doubt because Ava Carris was a live time bomb.

The house on the far edge of the neighboring town of Dobson was small and white with a one-car garage. She could see how Ava had managed to seemingly disappear. Dobson was a tiny town, with little more than an independent convenience store and a school.

The deputy was waiting for her with the owner of the house, a tiny, elderly man who was full of questions about why the sheriff was looking for such a sweet woman.

"What could she have possibly done, a little, meek thing like her?" the owner said.

McCall asked him to open the door and please wait for them outside.

"You aren't going to try to tell me this woman is dangerous," he said with a laugh, then sobered as he caught the look the sheriff and deputy exchanged before pulling their weapons and stepping inside.

The interior of the house was as McCall would have expected. Small, old and scented with that unique smell closed-up old houses always had. The furniture was minimal as they moved through the living room, checked the one bedroom and bath before entering the kitchen.

In here, the smell was convenience-store fast food. Several bags were in the garbage can by the back door.

McCall spotted a paper bag on the floor by the table and stepped toward it, stopping short when she saw the knife lying on the floor in the shadow of the table.

"See what else you can find," she told her deputy as she holstered her weapon and pulled out an evidence bag and latex gloves. She bagged the bloody knife, then looked around. Why would Ava leave this just lying here?

McCall reminded herself that she wasn't dealing with a necessarily logical-thinking woman. As she stepped into the bedroom, the deputy motioned to the closet and the suitcase open on the floor next to it.

"She was either packing or moving in," he said.

McCall would guess packing, assuming that for some reason she'd left in a hurry since she'd apparently been stopped in the middle of the job.

She moved to the end table beside the bed. A stack of vacation brochures from the area cluttered the small scarred table.

"Did you find any sign that Kayley has been here?" he asked.

Something caught her eye.

"Did you find something?" the deputy asked.

McCall carefully picked up one of the brochures about Montana's history. Someone had circled a section about some old gold mines.

Why would Ava Carris be interested in gold mines?

"Where are the closest old gold mines around here?" she asked the deputy.

"Used to be a lot of gold in the Little Rockies."

McCall remembered when the mines had shut down about ten years ago. Everyone had thought Whitehorse would wither and die because the town had become so dependent on the money the miners spent.

Whitehorse, even though it was an hour away, had been the closest town, where everyone had shopped for groceries and supplies. People joked about the last person in town turning out the lights on their way out.

"You know there's those old mines north of town just up from the river," the deputy said.

"Near the Dennison ranch." McCall felt the hair rise on the back of her neck. Since she'd joined the sheriff's department, she'd worked on instinct. "Let's close up here. I want you to park somewhere inconspicuous and watch the house. I think I'll go check those mines."

She could tell the deputy thought she was the one with the screw loose as she left. Who hid out in an old, dangerous mine tunnel on a cold, snowy, late-November day?

She knew it was a long shot. But Ava Carris had circled the story. Add to that the fact that the mines weren't far from Jace Dennison's house.

JACE TOOK THE BACK WAY, not surprised to see that Ava had done the same thing. That explained how he'd missed her. She couldn't have left Kayley's house much before he had, and yet he hadn't seen her on the highway.

He realized with a start that this hadn't been impulsive. She had planned this, scoped out the area, decided where she was going to take Kayley. She would have seen the mine tunnel from the photographs of him and Kayley in the albums at the house, recognized the location and possibly even explored the mines.

Which meant she had the home-field advantage.

Jace tried not to think about what Ava hoped to gain out of this—or how far she would go as he drove down the narrow, snowy road. What scared him was the struggle he'd heard before the phone had gone dead.

He'd tried to call back but got voice mail. He prayed Kayley was still alive as he followed the single set of tracks up the road toward the large bare-limbed cottonwoods that stood stark against the snowy landscape. It was there that the road ended—at the Milk River.

This part of the valley had gotten a lot less snow and while it had still blown in some, the storm hadn't closed the road.

If the storm had been more extensive, Ava wouldn't have been able to get in even with a four-wheel-drive SUV; she would have high-centered on the drifts and had to abort her plan. Unfortunately, that hadn't happened.

As he drove in, he knew the sound of his uncle's pickup's engine would carry for miles along the river bottom. Ava would know that he was coming.

But she already knew he would come. That was why she'd taken Kayley. She knew his weakness. She'd read the letters his mother had saved from Kayley, including the ones that mentioned the baby she and Jace had lost. She'd seen the photographs of the two of them. She had been more aware of his heart's desire than he had.

Now, though, he had to believe that she wouldn't hurt Kayley. That the person she really wanted was him.

The road ended at the fishing-access site in a stand of huge cottonwoods. Deep in the shadows sat a silver SUV.

Jace parked next to the SUV and got out, dragging the backpack he'd brought with him. For a moment, he stood looking toward the mountainside. The mines had been dug into the side of a cliff overlooking the Milk River back in the early 1900s during a late gold rush. A narrow trail led up to the first opening.

This spot was a popular fishing-access site in the summer, but no one used it this time of year. Jace figured it was why Ava had chosen the mine. There was little chance anyone would stumble on to her. And since there'd been only the one set of vehicle tracks in, now it was just him and Ava.

The wind whipped the branches over his head and moaned across the top of the vehicles, sending a shower of snow into the air. He saw no sign of Ava or Kayley, but he could see where they had made a trail through the fallen snow. The tracks had blown in, but there was still a shallow shadowed indentation where they'd walked.

Figuring Ava was watching him from the darkness beyond the partially barred entrance to the mine tunnel, he started up the trail. He knew Kayley was with Ava in the mine. Ava must have gone into the mine to get her for the phone call. That was good. It meant they hadn't ventured far into the mine, where anything could set off a cave-in.

He thought of the narrow, cramped tunnel inside, could almost feel the cold rock walls and imagine Kayley's fear. Had Ava now taken her deeper into the tunnel?

In his mind, he tried to picture the maze of tunnels inside the mine. He remembered the main tunnel forked: to the right the tunnel went upward: to the left it dropped deeper into the mountainside into a honeycomb of tunnels.

The ground was so unstable that a portion of the mine had caved in years ago, leaving a cavernous hole where the ground had given away above the upper tunnel, dropping into the lower ones.

If Ava took the right fork, he didn't have to worry about Kayley having enough oxygen, since the tunnel ended in a cliff with blue sky above it from where the ground had given way.

The problem was that the tunnel ended in a cliff—the drop to the rocks below was a good fifty feet.

But if Ava had taken the lower tunnel, it would eventually end in a wall of rock because of the old cave-in.

Jace hated to think where Kayley was being held. Anywhere beyond the entrance was bad. The deeper Ava took her in the tunnels, the harder it would be to get her out safely. That's if he could find her in that maze inside the mountain.

And if she was still alive.

He smacked that thought away. He had to stay focused. It wouldn't be the first time he'd gone into a situation knowing little about what he would be up against until he got there. The difference was there'd never been this much at stake.

Before, it had been only his own life he was jeopardizing. With all his other covert operations, the expected outcome was bad, because he wasn't called in unless there was little to no hope of getting the person out alive.

It was part of the job. There were always losses, because he wasn't called in unless all other alternatives had failed. But failure was not an option in this case.

He tried the cell-phone number again. No answer. He could see the mine opening just ahead. Behind what few boards still blocked the entrance, all he could see was darkness.

"Ava!" he called as he pulled the .357 from the holster. "Ava!" She either wasn't answering or she was deeper in the tunnel.

He moved cautiously. Standing to one side of the opening so he wasn't silhouetted in the entrance, he pulled the headlamp from his backpack, slipped it on and snapped on the light.

Then he stepped through the space between the boards, ducking his head as he entered the mine.

The inside of the mine was cold, damp and cramped. Each footfall echoed through the tunnel. Jace had gone only a few yards inside when he'd stopped to listen. He could hear water dripping somewhere ahead and feel a breeze against his face.

Cautiously, he moved deeper into the mountainside. The tunnel was narrow. In places he had to bend down to clear the rocky crags overhead. He and his uncle Audie had gone in a few hundred yards—to the point where one tunnel went down and the other went a little to the right and upward.

"Bad deal," Audie had said, shaking his head. "That lower tunnel will weaken the earth under the other. If it hasn't already caved in, it will."

They had taken the high tunnel but hadn't gone much farther when his uncle whispered for him to stay back. Jace had felt the fresh air on his face and known even before he reached his uncle that there had been a cave-in from overhead.

What surprised him was that the earth had dropped into the lower tunnel, leaving a crater, the ragged rocky edge high above as if a hole had been punched in the sky.

He and his uncle had turned back, with Audie eliciting a promise from him that he would never enter the mine again.

Jace had kept that promise. Until today.

As he reached the fork where the tunnels diverged, he saw a piece of cloth stuck in the rocks and recognized it as a strip of fabric from a shirt Kayley had been wearing just a few days before.

His heart pounded at the sight of it and the realization of which tunnel it marked. Weapon in hand, he took the higher tunnel—the one with the piece of cloth marking it—knowing that it ended abruptly on a ledge of unstable ground with a deadly fall to the rocks below.

He stopped again to listen, hoping to hear voices or the scuff of a shoe on the tunnel floor. All he could hear was the pounding of his own heart. He moved forward, his headlamp cutting a swath through the darkness ahead.

The tunnel turned. Jace bent to go under a low-hanging rock.

She came out of the darkness like a ghost, startling him not only by her sudden appearance, but also by the look on her face.

He straightened as the tunnel ceiling opened a little. "Ava." His voice sounded funny to him. It echoed around him. "Ava, where is Kayley?'

She stood at the edge of the cave-in, light spilling in from the opening to the sky. He realized what had startled him was the frightened look on her face.

Jace was doing his best to remain calm and patient, but he wasn't sure how much longer he could hold it together. "Ava, what did you do with her? Is she all right?"

"Evie has her. She's my identical twin sister. That's how she knew about Kayley. I told her Kayley wasn't a threat, but I've never been able to keep secrets from her."

Jace took a step toward her. Ava took a step back. He stopped, realizing how close she was to the edge of the cliff. He had to know what she'd done with Kayley.

"Evie doesn't have her. Your sister Eva is dead. She died when you were born."

Ava shook her head adamantly. "Papa just said she was dead. She was dead to him because she defied him when we were both fifteen, but Evie's not dead. Remember how she was always around, and you used to get so tired of it, John? You used to say—"

"Ava, you have to listen to me. I'm not John. I need to find Kayley. You have to help me."

"Evie—"

He was losing his patience. Every minute they were in this tunnel, the less chance they had of getting out of here without causing a cave-in. "Take me to Evie. If she has Kayley—"

"It wasn't my fault," she said in a little-girl voice.

His heart dropped. "What wasn't your fault?"

She cocked her head to one side, her eyes filling with tears. "Eva took her down the other tunnel. I think it caved in."

Jace swallowed hard. Kayley had to be all right. If he could just find her quickly… "Ava, I need you to go with me."

She looked and sounded like a little girl. "I can't. Evie will hurt me, too. I always get blamed for what she does," Ava cried, closing her eyes as she shook her head from side to side. "She does horrible things. Horrible things."

Jace reached for her, needing her to lead him to the spot where she'd last seen Kayley, but Ava took a step back, now just inches from where the tunnel floor ended and the earth dropped away to end fifty feet below in a pile of rocks.

"Ava," he said, lowering his voice. "Just show me where Kayley is. I will help you. I will make sure that Eva gets the blame for everything. I will protect you from her."

She opened her eyes and smiled ruefully. "No one can protect me from my sister."

"Ava, you're not like her. You're a nice person. I know you didn't hurt Kayley."

"I wouldn't hurt anyone. I only followed you because I thought…" She looked confused. "Evie said you are John come back from the dead. I knew you weren't, but I missed him so much. John loved me. He never loved Evie. He always wished she would go away and never come back."

Suddenly her head jerked to the side. Her eyes widened in alarm, and he could see that she was listening to something. Someone.

"Ava, what's wrong?"

Suddenly, her gaze swung to a spot just over his right shoulder. Her eyes widened in terror.

"Ava—"

When she opened her mouth, her voice was an eerie whisper. "Evie. She's right behind you."

Jace felt the hair rise on the nape of his neck as he swung around.

Chapter Thirteen

Jace turned and came face-to-face Eva Carris.

He knew at once she was the woman he'd met that night at the bar in Whitehorse.

"Hello, Jace," she said, smiling.

His heart hammered against his rib cage as he looked into the woman's eyes. She was identical to Ava—except for the eyes. There was something so cold and dangerous in them that he felt chilled to his bone marrow.

He held the .357 Magnum on her, his finger itching on the trigger.

"Where is Kayley?" he demanded, trying not to let her see just how shaken he was. Or how terrified of what he knew this woman was capable of.

Behind him, he could hear Ava whimpering like a puppy.

"I didn't tell him anything, Evie. I didn't. I did just as you said. I just stood here and waited for him like you said."

Eva sent her twin a look of disgust before she settled her gaze on Jace again.

"You aren't going to shoot me," she said. "If you do, you'll never find your precious Kayley. At least not until it's too late."

"What do you want?" he demanded, never taking the weapon off her.

"I like a man who gets right to the heart of the problem," Eva said. "What do I want?" She smiled, her eyes darkening with a twisted sickness. If he hadn't known it before, he did now. Here was a woman who loved tormenting others—especially her twin.

"I want you to kill my sister," Eva said.

Jace shook his head. "I'd rather kill you."

Behind him, Ava had let out a gasp at her sister's words.

An instant later, he heard her lose her footing. He swung around in time to see her off balance on the edge of the precipice.

She windmilled her arms frantically as she tried to regain her balance. He lunged for her, saw the change in her expression, the acceptance, the relief, as if she suddenly welcomed what was about to happen.

His fingers brushed hers as she fell. He dropped to the edge, still grasping for her, but she was gone. She didn't make a sound, even when she hit the rocks below.

Jace turned away in horror, a cold silence rushing in that was broken only by the soft click of the safety being snapped off on a pistol directly behind his ear.

MCCALL GOT THE CALL AS she left White-horse, headed north. She checked and saw that it was the retired detective from the John Carris case in Alaska and was marked urgent.

"Sheriff Winchester," he said, sounding upset when she answered.

"I have a homicide down here and a possible hostage situation," McCall told him. She'd just driven by Kayley's after not being able to reach Jace and seen where there had been a struggle. "A rancher who was drugged, then stabbed eleven times. The last person he was seen with matches Ava Carris's description. I have an APB out on her. I suspect she has taken the local hostage to an old gold mine. I'm going there now."

"It might not have been Ava," the former detective said. "That's why I called you. Her twin sister is alive."

McCall felt her blood run cold. "I thought—"

"Ava's father showed up at the police station yesterday. He said he was afraid of his daughter. Of course the detective in charge thought he meant Ava. That's when he admitted that he had lied when social services had come around all those years ago. Eva had run off when she was fifteen. He'd literally buried her memory in the backyard. Apparently she's been living with him off and on for years. She came and went, but he had become worried about her, fearing she might want to harm her sister. He said she was always jealous of Ava."

"Why would he make such a confession now?" McCall asked.

"He said he'd heard from Eva and that she'd threatened to come home soon. According to him, Eva told him that she was taking care of Ava and from now on she would be living as her sister. He said that Eva had always been filled with sin. He had tried to beat it out of her but had failed."

McCall cursed under her breath.

"Sheriff, the district attorney up here was planning to reopen the case against Ava Carris in the murder of her husband. With the twin sister being alive, this sheds a whole new light on everything we know about Ava Carris."

McCall thanked him, promising to keep him informed.

The moment she hung up, she called Jace's number. No answer. She left a message for him to contact her immediately, that it was urgent, then slowed for the turnoff to the mines.

That's when she saw two sets of tracks going into the fishing-access road.

As she drove toward the river, she couldn't help but think about the ten years that Ava Carris had spent in a mental institution—and all because she'd sworn her sister had killed John Carris.

What if it had never been Ava who hurt anyone? What if it had been her sister, Eva, all along? Being twins, Eva could come and go at will as long as she made sure the two of them were never seen together.

When McCall saw the two vehicles parked at the end of the road, she put in a call to one of her deputies. "I'm headed for the old mines north of the Dennison place. I believe that we have four people inside." She gave the deputy the information about Ava Carris's twin, warning that both should be considered armed and dangerous at this point, and asked for backup.

Then she parked and, grabbing her shotgun, stepped out and began the hike up to the old mine entrance.

"ARE YOU INSANE?" Jace demanded as the report of the pistol set off a series of small cave-ins along the tunnel behind them.

Eva chuckled after firing the shot into the air. "Do I really need to answer that?" She pressed the barrel end of the pistol into the back of his head again.

He was still in shock that she would do that to her own sister. Her twin. "You killed her just as if you'd put that gun to her head."

"You think? Actually, I'm going to miss her. She was so much fun. But with her out of the sanitarium, it was causing a little problem. There can't be two of us. One of us has to be dead. Now, get up slowly. Remember, one wrong move and Kayley dies."

"How do I know she isn't dead already?" Jace asked as he slowly got to his feet. It was all he could do not to take that gun away from her and strangle the twisted life out of her.

The only thing that stopped him was that she was the only one who knew where Kayley was.

And yet he had a feeling she wasn't going to take him to Kayley. With him and Kayley and Ava dead, the sheriff would think this tragedy was over.

Eva had been able to come and go for years as Ava. Until Ava got out of the mental hospital.

Even if Eva got caught, she could blame all of this on Ava—just as she had always done, according to Ava.

As he stood and turned to face her—and the gun she was holding on him, he saw her sudden change of expression.

She tilted her head, looking surprised. Jace heard it, too. Someone calling for help. The voice distant and muffled. Jace knew then that Eva had reason to believe that Kayley was dead and that the only person who could be calling was her sister.

"It's Ava calling you," he said, even though he knew better. He'd seen where she'd landed in the rocks. No one could survive a fall like that.

But Eva didn't know that, and in the sudden fear he saw contort her face, he realized Ava hadn't been the only one haunted by her sister all these years.

He pretended to turn to look back over the edge of the precipice as if to call to Ava, his heart pounding with hope. Kayley was alive somewhere in this mine, and he was going to find her.

Just as he had anticipated, Eva stepped toward the dropoff, desperate now to see if her sister had survived.

Jace prayed he wasn't making the biggest mistake of his life as he swung his leg, catching Eva in the back of the head at the same time as he dove to the side.

She got one shot off before she went over the edge. Her scream was wild and primitive, echoing through the tunnel as dirt and rocks showered down from the gunshot blast.

When the scream ended as abruptly as it started, he quickly got to his feet.

He didn't need to look over the edge, but he did. The sisters lay side by side like two tiny broken dolls on the rocks fifty feet below.

Jace turned away, listening. He could hear Kayley calling to him from somewhere below in one of the lower tunnels.

"Kayley!" His voice echoed through the crater of rocks and back down the tunnel.

He waited, then heard her calling again. It was faint. He didn't call again, knowing that any sound could set off a cave-in. She would have heard the gunshots, Eva's horrible scream. Hopefully she would know he was finally coming for her.

MCCALL HAD REACHED THE entrance to the mine. She'd followed the fresh tracks in the snow and knew they had to be Jace Dennison's.

Her deputy had called her back just moments ago to tell her that Jace's rental SUV was parked at his house but that Audie's pickup was missing.

Not missing anymore, she thought.

When she'd seen the brochure with the mine circled at Ava Carris's rental house, McCall had feared that Kayley hadn't gotten out of town. Now she was even more concerned that was the case.

At the mine entrance, she had stopped to

listen, hearing nothing but a hawk crying out as it circled high overhead in a sky of blue.

Pulling out her flashlight, she'd snapped it on, then stepped through the opening into the tunnel.

Weapon in one hand and flashlight in the other, she'd moved deeper into the mine, afraid of what she was going to find.

She hadn't gone far when she'd heard the gunshot.

FOR A FEW MOMENTS KAYLEY couldn't remember where she was or what had happened. Her memory came back in a rush.

She and Ava had been descending deeper into the lower tunnel when it had started to cave in. Kayley had seen her chance and run— only to end up trapped on the other side of the cave-in.

A rock had hit her and knocked her down. She must have blacked out from the pain.

Now she tried to sit up to assess the damage but realized her ankle was caught under the rubble. When she tried to move it, she knew she wasn't going anywhere. She let out a cry of pain and frustration as she lay back.

The darkness was intense. She couldn't tell

what was up or down. She felt disoriented and felt herself start to panic. What if there wasn't enough air in this part of the chamber where she was now trapped?

Running into the cave-in had been a desperate measure. But she'd known after she talked to Jace on the phone that Ava didn't plan to keep her alive until he got there.

She'd seen the change in the woman, almost as if she were someone else, someone who had no respect for human life. It hadn't been anger in Ava's eyes—just a total lack of compassion.

Now, though, Kayley feared she'd played right into her kidnapper's hands. The thought made her angry with herself. She wasn't going to die in here. Well, at least she wasn't going to die without putting up a fight.

She pushed herself up as far as she could with the pain in her ankle nearly making her black out again and began to work at moving the debris off her injured leg.

It was slow work, but she was afraid to use too much oxygen too quickly. She tried to breathe normally as she moved the rocks and dirt until she could work her leg out by lifting it with both hands.

As she felt along the ankle, she knew it was broken. She'd expected to feel a bone jutting out given the amount of pain she was in.

But the break seemed to be a clean one. Taking off her jacket and shirt, she tore her shirt into wide strips to try to bind the break as best she could.

Kayley knew she wouldn't be able to stand, but she needed to be able to move if she hoped to get out of here.

Her heart broke at the thought that Jace was walking right into Ava's trap. She reminded herself that Jace was trained for dangerous undercover work. Unfortunately, he was still injured after his latest assignment. He'd been limping and when they'd made love, she'd seen the scar on his thigh that hadn't yet healed.

She just hoped he didn't make the mistake of underestimating Ava.

But she couldn't think about any of that. She had to concentrate on getting out of here and praying for Jace's safety.

After she had tied her ankle, she put her coat back on against the cold of the tunnel. Fortunately it was about forty degrees, warmer than outside.

Common sense told her that since she

couldn't walk, she would have to dig her way out. The cave-in hadn't been extensive, because she hadn't taken but a few steps before she'd been hit and knocked down.

She began to dig, dragging herself higher up the pile of small rocks and dirt.

She had stopped to rest for a moment when she thought she heard a gunshot. Her stomach dropped. Jace. Ava had killed him. She doubled over, unable to hold back the tears.

Another gunshot. She lifted her head. That's when she heard what could only be a horrible scream. A *woman's* scream.

"Jace!" She yelled as loud as she could. Then she thought she heard him answer, but she might only have imagined it.

Kayley began to dig as if her life depended on it. She had a bad feeling it did.

WHEN JACE REACHED THE fork in the mine tunnels, he took the lower one, following the winding narrow passageway deeper and deeper downward.

According to Ava there had been a cave-in, and Kayley had gotten caught in it.

But she was alive.

He'd heard her calling to him. No one could

tell him any different even if he questioned how he could have heard anything deep in this mine.

His mind raced. For him to be able to hear Kayley, it meant that she was in a tunnel that opened to the cavernous hole where Ava and Eva now lay. That made sense, and he knew that he had to be thinking logically right now. He couldn't let his emotions get in the way.

Ahead, he heard the frightening sound of small rocks and dirt cascading down. This old mine was ready to cave in at any moment.

The channel narrowed, and he had to stoop to see ahead. His light shone into the darkness, illuminating nothing but a solid wall of rock where the passage had caved in.

He quickly backtracked and took another tunnel, praying he was heading in the right direction.

Not far in, he saw that this one, too, had caved in.

His heart leaped when he heard what sounded like someone digging on the other side.

He quickly pulled the shovel from his backpack and went to work moving the earth and small rocks, telling himself Kayley was on the other side, digging just as frantically as he was. He told himself she would have enough air. The fact that he'd heard her calling meant there was an opening on the cavern at the end of this tunnel.

Still, Jace felt the clock ticking as he dug at the rock and dirt.

He moved another shovelful of earth. His light shone into a hole, and he saw her. Kayley. She was covered with dirt, her hands scraped and bleeding, tears in her eyes. He scrambled to make the hole larger until he could get through it.

He carefully drew her into his arms, seeing that she was in pain, her ankle bandaged with pieces of her shirt—the same shirt scrap that had marked the tunnel that had led him to Ava.

"Kayley, Kayley," he said into her hair.

She nestled against him, crying. "I was so worried about you," she kept saying. "I was so scared that she would kill you."

Jace heard a sound. A moment later, the light from a headlamp flickered over them, and minutes later Sheriff McCall Winchester was helping him get Kayley out of the tunnel and into the brilliant sunlight of the snowy late-November day.

Chapter Fourteen

Kayley lay in the hospital bed, watching the sun rise over the Montana prairie and studying the man sleeping in the chair beside her bed.

Jace Dennison was the most handsome man she'd ever known, but it was his heart that had always attracted her to him. No one could ever understand why she hadn't given up on him. She had weakened a few times recently.

But ultimately she'd prayed that she wouldn't lose him.

She and his mother used to spend hours talking about him, worrying about him, wanting him home. They had faith that Jace would come to his senses, as his mother used to say.

"You're the only woman for him, you have to know that, Kayley," Marie used to say. "But

I don't want you to wait for him. It's not fair to you."

"I'm not waiting for him," Kayley used to say, and they would both laugh because they knew it was a lie.

She looked at him now and was filled with so much love it felt as if she might burst from it. How could anyone love this much and not be consumed by it?

Her thoughts turned to Ava Carris. Had she loved her husband, John, like that?

Jace had filled her in last night on the way to the hospital. She'd been shocked at how his resemblance to Ava's deceased husband had set off this string of events that had ended with such tragedy at the mine.

Kayley's heart went out to Ava. Her own sister had taken the man she loved from her. No wonder Ava had latched on to the hope that a little of the man she had loved lived on in Jace Dennison.

If anyone knew that kind of undying love, it was Kayley.

JACE WOKE IN THE CHAIR next to Kayley's bed to see her smiling over at him.

"Good morning," he said, sitting up and stretching out the kinks.

"You didn't have to stay all night," she said. "That chair must have been horribly uncomfortable."

He grinned. "I've slept in worse places. Anyway, I wasn't leaving your side."

"Well, you're going to have to. The doctor just stopped by. He's coming back to check me over. He's letting me go home."

"I'm taking you home."

"Jace—"

He stepped to the bed and placed a finger on her lips. "Kayley, you've stopped me every time I wanted to tell you how I feel about you. Not this time."

She looked at him, her gaze solemn.

"I am so thankful you're all right." His voice broke.

"Thanks to you," she said. "If you hadn't gotten to me when you did—"

"I love you. I've never stopped loving you. I should never have left you. I'm never going to again."

"Jace, we've both been through a lot. This isn't the time to make a decision you'll regret later."

"I'd decided I couldn't go through with selling the place. I didn't want to. I couldn't leave you again. All I could think about was seeing you when you got back from Billings, and then I got the call from Ava."

"Jace—"

"Kayley, please let me say this. I'm going to prove to you that I'm worthy of your love and trust. I was so devastated when my father died, that when we lost the baby it was as if my world had shattered. I felt so helpless and afraid."

"We both did, Jace."

"I know that now, but back then you seemed so strong, so sure of things. I wasn't. You wanted to start a family right away after we were married. I was scared of losing another baby or, worse, losing you. I didn't want to love anyone that much ever again."

She nodded and cupped his face with her bandaged hand.

"I thought I would be safe with the life I chose because there was no chance of ever feeling like that again," he continued, needing to get this out. "The only life I would be risking was my own. But I never got over you. I told myself that if I didn't see you... Later,

I couldn't face you after what I'd done. I left you to grieve for our baby alone. I abandoned you."

"Jace, I knew how hard it was for you. I felt your pain."

"What about your own, Kayley?"

She smiled at him. "I knew you loved me. That got me through it."

He shook his head. "You are the most amazing woman."

"No, I'm not, Jace. I just believed in our love and tried not to give up hope that one day you would come back. Really come back."

"Well, I'm back now," he said and kissed her.

VIRGINIA HEARD ABOUT what had happened the way most news moved in Whitehorse County—the grapevine. She'd been so upset she'd called her niece.

"Is Jace all right?" Virginia had asked the sheriff the moment McCall answered.

"He's fine. Kayley has a broken ankle. Doc kept her overnight to make sure she was all right, but I just heard they are letting her go home today."

And Jace would be leaving again.

"Jace saved her life," McCall said. "Somehow he found her in one of the deepest tunnels. He swears he heard her calling him. It would have been impossible that deep in the mountain even with an opening farther down the tunnel."

Virginia felt sad that her son had apparently taken after both his biological parents. "How can he not realize that Kayley is the woman he should be with?"

"He's a man. Sometimes it takes a tragedy to make them see the truth. Maybe this has done that for him."

"I hope so. I don't want him to spend his life alone." *Like his mother did,* Virginia thought. "I thought I lost my son. When you lose a child, especially if you're alone or at least feel that you're alone, it changes something in you. You are terrified of feeling that kind of pain again."

"Have you seen him?" McCall asked.

Virginia smiled to herself, remembering the night she'd stopped by Jace's home. It hadn't gone the way she'd hoped it would, but she'd gotten to spend a little time with her son. She could go years on just that.

"Yes," she said. "I got to see him and talk to him. I'm okay now."

PEPPER WINCHESTER HADN'T been able to forget her only daughter's request. She'd always feared that Virginia was selfish, greedy, heartless—just like everyone thought Pepper herself was.

But it wasn't until the two of them had spent time here on the ranch recently that she'd realized her daughter was more like her than she'd ever wanted to admit. Virginia hid her feelings, coming off as cold and uncaring. Pepper knew the feeling well.

Like her, Virginia had been hurt badly. She had locked herself away, as well. While her daughter hadn't become a recluse for the past twenty-seven years, she had sealed herself off from the world with a mask of bitterness and anger.

It had taken Jace Dennison and the knowledge that her son was alive to open her heart.

Pepper had seen the change in Virginia but had still been surprised when her daughter had asked her to acknowledge Jace as her grandson and give her share of the Winchester fortune to him rather than her.

It was then that Pepper realized just how much Virginia had changed. For the first time, she had hope that her daughter might actually find some happiness in this life.

Now, as she picked up the phone, the matriarch of the Winchester ranch felt a strange sense of hope herself.

Jace Dennison answered on the third ring.

"You don't know me," Pepper said. "But I'm your grandmother, and I want to invite you out to the ranch. I know you are probably not ready. But if you ever are, the door is open."

"Thank you," he said. "I—"

"You don't have to explain," she said and actually chuckled. "If anyone understands how hard it is to be a Winchester, it is me. You take care of yourself." She hung up, then picked up the phone and called her new lawyer to draft a new will.

KAYLEY INSISTED THEY take it slow. She was getting around her house fine on crutches now that she was out of the hospital, and she definitely didn't want Jace waiting on her hand and foot.

She'd sent him back to his own house just up the road.

"I have to get back in my classroom," she told him. "No matter what happens with us, I want to keep teaching. At least for a while." She meant until they had children, but she didn't want to put any pressure on Jace. He had things he needed to take care of, like adjusting to the idea of staying in Whitehorse.

Ava's and Eva's bodies had been taken out of the old mine by airlift, their ashes sent back to Alaska for what their father called a proper burial.

It snowed the day of Ty Reynolds's funeral. Kayley stood next to Jace. The entire county had turned out, everyone saying what a nice guy Ty had been.

"You can't blame yourself," she'd told Jace after the funeral, knowing that he did. "Ty was the one who picked up Eva that night in the bar. Nor was it your fault that you resembled Ava's husband."

"That's what's so weird," Jace said. "McCall got a photograph of John Carris. We really look nothing alike."

That was odd, Kayley thought. Ava must have seen something in Jace, a kindness in his face, a compassion, or even his pain, something that had drawn her to him—and Whitehorse.

"Maybe it was always supposed to end here," Kayley said making Jace laugh. She did love the sound of his laugh.

"Are you telling me it was fate?"

She thought of Marie. "Something like that."

Jace nodded, his gaze caressing her face. "Maybe you're right."

JACE REALIZED THAT AS strange and tragic as it was, Ava and Eva had brought him and Kayley together again. Life did work in mysterious ways.

He took solace in the fact that Ava was at peace. Eva, well, he wouldn't count on that.

Since taking Kayley home from the hospital, Jace had been busy getting his life in order. He'd taken the For Sale sign out of the yard and called his boss. He wouldn't be going back. His boss tried to change his mind, but Jace finally knew what he wanted. There would be other, younger men eager to save the world.

His place was in Whitehorse, Montana.

He'd finally quit running.

But that meant there was one thing he had to do.

One day in the weeks before Christmas, he

drove south through the snowy rolling prairie. It was another of those brilliant winter days when the sun glistens on the snow and the sky is an incredible blinding blue.

In the distance, the Little Rockies were a deep purple. Only a few clouds bobbed along in that sea of blue. Several bald eagles watched him drive by from their perches in the bare limbs of a tree silhouetted against the horizon.

Jace had never been to the Winchester ranch, but then again few people had in the past twenty-seven years.

As he drove under the log arch, he thought of his mother. Jace knew Marie would have approved of what he was about to do. That made him feel a little better.

For years Kayley wasn't the only one who'd been waiting, believing one day he would come home to the woman he loved and this place and lifestyle he'd once loved more than life itself.

His mother had faith that he would eventually quit running from the pain of his loss and his fears and risk that kind of loss again for love.

As he came over a rise, he saw the ranch lodge. The log structure looked old and very western. He'd heard the lodge had been built back in the 1940s, designed after the famous Old Faithful Lodge in Yellowstone Park.

According to the stories, patriarch Call Winchester had amassed a fortune and built the lodge onto an older section his parents had constructed years before.

He'd added the adjacent barns and outbuildings and bought up more land until he had one of the largest ranches in the county.

As Jace got out, the front door opened and he saw Virginia Winchester standing in the doorway.

The look on her face threatened to break his heart. She looked so happy to see him. He wondered for a moment if coming out here wasn't a mistake. He wasn't sure he was ready for this.

Then he reminded himself of his promise not to close himself off from the people who cared about him and walked toward the lodge and his mother.

Chapter Fifteen

With Christmas and her wedding just weeks away, Sheriff McCall Winchester knew she couldn't put it off any longer.

The whole family would be attending the wedding. She had to find out if someone in the family had been involved in her father's death. She knew her grandmother had been doing some investigating of her own. As far as McCall could tell, though, Pepper hadn't discovered who might have betrayed not only McCall's father, but also Pepper herself.

"She's never going to let it lie," McCall told her fiancé, Luke Crawford, as they lay in the small double bed in his travel trailer.

Through the window, she could see the beautiful house he'd built for them. Luke said it would be finished by the time they returned from their honeymoon and had made her promise she wouldn't peek inside until then.

She couldn't have been more excited—and anxious about marrying this man lying next to her.

"Are we talking about your grandmother again?" he asked, sounding half-asleep.

"I'm worried about the wedding." She knew they'd had this discussion many times before. When her grandmother had insisted she and Luke get married at the Winchester ranch, McCall had been touched. After all, except for a few months of her life, she'd been the black sheep, an outcast, not even accepted as a Winchester, her paternity in question.

All that had changed when she'd discovered that her father, Trace Winchester, had never left town on the lam, leaving behind a pregnant wife and a devastated mother. His murder had brought his daughter and mother together.

The second shock to both of them was how much McCall resembled her grandmother.

"The problem is that Pepper is still convinced someone in the family was involved in Trace's murder," she told her fiancé now.

Luke opened one eye and focused it on her.

"I wondered how long it would take before you admitted you agree with her."

"Who said I agree?"

Luke laughed and closed his eye again. "Your grandmother is right. You make a damned good sheriff. You're a born investigator. So investigate. Better to find out before the wedding, don't you think?"

She lay back on her pillow, staring up at the ceiling. "There isn't much time," she said, more to herself than Luke. "But the whole family is coming home a few days before the wedding."

McCall sighed. Why had she been putting it off?

Because her father was dead and nothing could bring him back. And investigating her own family, the family she'd just been accepted into, wasn't something she'd wanted to do. A sure sign she shouldn't be sheriff.

As she studied the trailer ceiling, she had to admit the truth to herself. She believed that the killer hadn't acted alone, had suspected it from the moment she'd found her father's remains within sight of the Winchester ranch. There had only been one reason to kill her father on that high ridge with the ranch in the distance.

And while she was being truthful, she wasn't sure she wanted to know who in the Winchester family had been involved. She feared her grandmother would regret knowing, as well.

But the wedding day was looming. It was time to find out who in the wedding party was an accomplice to murder.

Chapter Sixteen

Kayley heard the sound of a pickup coming up the drive and looked out to see Jace pull up and get out of his uncle's truck.

As he reached in the back, she caught a glimpse of evergreen. To her delight, he pulled out a Christmas tree. With everything that had been going on, she hadn't had time to even think about Christmas, let alone a tree. Not that she could go out and cut one with her ankle in a cast—even a walking cast.

As Jace started for the house, he spotted her at the window. He smiled and mouthed "I love you."

She felt that surge of warmth that always filled her at the sight of him. She hobbled to the door and opened it, letting him and the tree in on a gust of cold air.

"I know you like to go get your own tree

every year, but since you can't, I went out and cut you one. I hope you like it."

"That was very thoughtful."

He grinned at her, that melting grin of his. "I was hoping we could decorate it together. Like we used to."

She nodded, smiling. Over the past few weeks, they hadn't spent a lot of time together. She'd been busy with school, and he had been busy at his place.

"I'd like that," Kayley said, remembering all the other Christmases they had decorated not only the tree at her house, but at his, as well. "I have some hot apple cider on the stove, and I made another batch of gingerbread men."

He breathed in the scent. "Yum. It smells great in here."

While Jace set up the tree, Kayley put Christmas music on the stereo and dug out the boxes of Christmas ornaments.

Outside it had begun to snow, huge white flakes that floated by on the wind. They were definitely going to have a white Christmas. She loved these kinds of snowstorms. There was something so pure in the cold silence of falling snow.

Inside, they decorated the tree, each ornament bringing back memories and stories they relived together. They laughed and recalled moments with his mother, Marie, who had always loved Christmas.

When they'd finished, it was dark out. Kayley turned out the house lights, and Jace plugged in the tree. The sight brought tears to her eyes.

"It's beautiful," she whispered as Jace took her hand and they sat on the floor under it looking up at it just as they had when they were kids. It felt like the time she'd seen her first Christmas tree and known there would be many more to come.

"Thank you, Jace. You couldn't have given me something I wanted more."

"It is beautiful. Just like you."

She looked over at him. Love shone in his dark eyes. He'd come home to her. There was no doubt in her mind now. Jace Dennison was finally where he belonged. By her side.

"I have something else for you," he said.

"Jace, it isn't Christmas yet."

"It's a little pre-Christmas surprise." He reached into his pocket and brought out a small velvet box.

Her heart began to pound. "Jace—"

"Please, just open it."

She took the box in trembling fingers, then slowly opened it and felt her heart lift like helium. There, nestled in the box, was the engagement ring he'd given her twelve years ago. The same one she'd given back the day he left Whitehorse.

"You once said that you loved this ring. Do you still love it?" he asked.

She threw her arms around his neck, unable to hold back the tears.

He got on both knees in front of her, the two of them sitting in the twinkling lights of the Christmas tree. "Kayley Mitchell, will you marry me?"

She looked into his dark eyes and saw nothing but love. Jace Dennison really was home— and hers. "Yes. Oh, yes."

Jace slipped the ring onto her finger, a perfect fit. "I love you, Kayley. I want to spend the rest of my life with you."

As she curled up in his arms beside the tree, Christmas music playing softly and the smell of cider and gingerbread cookies in the air, Kayley decided to keep her little surprise until Christmas.

* * * * *

LARGER-PRINT BOOKS!

GET 2 FREE LARGER-PRINT NOVELS
PLUS 2 FREE GIFTS!

Breathtaking Romantic Suspense

YES! Please send me 2 FREE LARGER-PRINT Harlequin Intrigue® novels and my 2 FREE gifts (gifts are worth about $10). After receiving them, if I don't wish to receive any more books, I can return the shipping statement marked "cancel." If I don't cancel, I will receive 6 brand-new novels every month and be billed just $4.99 per book in the U.S. or $5.74 per book in Canada. That's a saving of at least 13% off the cover price! It's quite a bargain! Shipping and handling is just 50¢ per book.* I understand that accepting the 2 free books and gifts places me under no obligation to buy anything. I can always return a shipment and cancel at any time. Even if I never buy another book from Harlequin, the two free books and gifts are mine to keep forever.

199/399 HDN E5MS

Name _____ (PLEASE PRINT) _____

Address _____ Apt. # _____

City _____ State/Prov. _____ Zip/Postal Code _____

Signature (if under 18, a parent or guardian must sign)

Mail to the **Harlequin Reader Service:**
IN U.S.A.: P.O. Box 1867, Buffalo, NY 14240-1867
IN CANADA: P.O. Box 609, Fort Erie, Ontario L2A 5X3

Not valid for current subscribers to Harlequin Intrigue Larger-Print books.

Are you a subscriber to Harlequin Intrigue books and want to receive the larger-print edition? Call 1-800-873-8635 today!

* Terms and prices subject to change without notice. Prices do not include applicable taxes. N.Y. residents add applicable sales tax. Canadian residents will be charged applicable provincial taxes and GST. Offer not valid in Quebec. This offer is limited to one order per household. All orders subject to approval. Credit or debit balances in a customer's account(s) may be offset by any other outstanding balance owed by or to the customer. Please allow 4 to 6 weeks for delivery. Offer available while quantities last.

Your Privacy: Harlequin Books is committed to protecting your privacy. Our Privacy Policy is available online at www.eHarlequin.com or upon request from the Reader Service. From time to time we make our lists of customers available to reputable third parties who may have a product or service of interest to you. If you would prefer we not share your name and address, please check here. ☐

Help us get it right—We strive for accurate, respectful and relevant communications. To clarify or modify your communication preferences, visit us at www.ReaderService.com/consumerschoice.

HILP10R

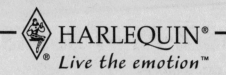